God's medicine-men
& other stories

malthouse African fiction

God's medicine-men & other stories

by

Tanure Ojaide

malthouse 𝄞

Malthouse Press Limited
Lagos, Benin, Ibadan, Jos, Oxford, Zaria

Malthouse Press Limited
11B Goriola Street, Off Adeola Odeku, Victoria Island, Lagos
E-mail: malthouse_press@yahoo.com
Tel: 01-773 53 44, 01-613 957, 0802 364 2402

Lagos Benin Ibadan Jos Oxford Port-Harcourt Zaria

© Tanure Ojaide 2004

First Published 2004

ISBN 978 023 137 4

Distributors:
African Books Collective Ltd
Oxford , United Kingdom

Tel: +44 - (0) 1865 -726686
Fax: +44 - (0) 1865 -793298
Email: abc@africanbookscollective.com
Website: http://www.africanbookscollective.com

dedication

to:

Joe Ewubare who challenged me to tell stories.

acknowledgements

I am specially grateful to Odun Balogun who meticulously read these stories and offered me suggestions that made me to understand better the craft of the short story.

the stories

Note: All stories are fictitious and names of characters have no bearing with people who might have similar names.

come back when you are ready to die

My mother was not all that old. At sixty-eight or thereabouts she was strong. Therefore her sudden deterioration from what appeared to be a common ailment alarmed all of us, the more so after the doctors at Eku Baptist Hospital, the best hospital in the area, had told us not to worry about her condition. At first the doctors diagnosed fatigue, exacerbated by malaria. Almost everybody once in a while suffered from malaria which incapacitated one for a week or so and then one bounced back.

My mother had asked to be taken to hospital because she did not like the way she felt. She was a hard worker who never complained of fatigue. It was rare for any ailment to weaken her to the extent of preventing her from going to farm or the market. Hence when I was informed that Mother wanted to be taken to the hospital, I knew that she had a premonition about something terrible happening to her. I began to understand the full impact of her remark when of recent I had visited. She told me to always look back, which was her cryptic way of saying that I should not be too far away in case she might need me.

At the hospital, I spent many hours by her sick bed and her voice was as strong and penetrating as ever.

"One doesn't know when the tree will fall," she told me.

I nodded. What else could I say to such words of deep foreboding? She got up on her own to go to the toilet and refused help of the nurses. This encouraged me to think about when she would be discharged, a thought that was further strengthened by the fact that she was unusually cheerful when she started the story that she insisted on telling me that night, the third night of her hospitalization. She, however, interrupted the real story to make what I considered to be unrelated comments.

"When you think the tree is strong, then comes the hurricane to knock it down," she said.

We live in a rain-forest area where hurricanes harass us during much of the rainy season. True, branches get torn from trees all the time; and in other cases, the trees themselves fall. I am not used to speaking in proverbs but I found an opportunity to calm her with these wise words:

"Mother, you don't have to worry. You know a tree with many branches will never hit the ground."

"That's true, my son. Who could have thought that I, the only child of my mother and for long believed to be barren, would have all of you? Yes, I am now a big tree with many branches; that's why I am happy," she commented.

"You are almost well already, so don't be afraid," I advised.

"I cannot be afraid. I have surprised myself in my life. Whether I become well or not, don't cry when I die," she said.

"But you are not going to die," I told her as if I was God.

"Sooner or later the tree will fall," she insisted.

After she completed telling me her story, our story, on that third night, I went home very late. I felt that she had passed the worst stage of her sickness and would soon be out of hospital. Restless as she had always been, I thought she would ask for her discharge even before I arrived the following day.

The following morning when I arrived at the hospital, she had died. The nurses did not even know until some twenty minutes before my arrival. They had wanted to give her the tablets she needed and found her still sleeping, or so they thought. The nurse who approached her screamed in response to the sight of her body, and other nurses soon came. They called a doctor to examine her. In my presence, she was pronounced dead.

* * *

There are orders which are too difficult to obey. I cried at her death, even though I recalled her advice that I should not. In Agbon, it is said that you can borrow money to celebrate a great festival. After the festival in which you have lavishly treated your guests, you work hard to recuperate your expenditure. Fortunately, I did not borrow, but you will know why I went to such length to make her posthumously proud after you hear the story she had told me the night before her death.

"I was the only child of my mother and my mother wasn't my father's favourite wife."

This was how she began her story.

"My father was rich, but preferred to marry more wives than to send his children to school. Out of the envy that he had for other men who sent their sons to school and in an effort to ward off scorn from the towns-people, my father reluctantly sent his older boys to school. Late or not, the boys went, but not the girls.

"I cried that I wanted to go to school as well, but my father's heart was rock-set on leaving me along with his other daughters at home. A few girls were going to school in the village and I liked their uniform, but ready as I was, I was never myself given this opportunity.

"At home, I was responsible for going to the farm, fetching water and firewood, washing clothes, and cooking. And, of course, all I had to do was to wait until I was married off.

"Today I cannot read or write. I could not learn that magic. But I swore from the beginning that I would someday make up for this deprivation. Our elders say that if you don't own something and that thing is in your house, it is still yours. You have graduated from the university, Ese and Ejiro are now there; others will follow. You see, I can say that I can read and write because you, my children, can read and write. You have even gone farther in your studies than the boys my father had sent to school.

"I learnt from my mother the will to succeed without help. If you are handicapped, you have to get to the fruiting tree before the able-bodied. That was my reasoning, because, as the daughter of a woman who was not her husband's favourite wife, I was very handicapped. My mother had to try many trades to feed me, herself, and sometimes even my father. He married the women to serve him. My mother was among the first women in Urhobo to tap rubber. She also had big cassava and yam farms. All my father did was to point at a jungle to the women and tell them, 'That portion is yours, that yours, and that yours and they knew what to do to fend for themselves. After all, they had children and did not have to wait for a husband to feed them. 'In this world, don't allow anybody to kill your hope,' my mother always told me. 'Don't let anybody feel sorry for you. Work hard and persist and you will succeed,' she advised me.

At sixteen years of age, I was given in marriage to a man from Agbarha, the town of only kings and queens. I was excited. What young lady would not be happy to be betrothed at that time when there was nothing ahead for girls other than marriage? If you stayed too long before marrying, people began to wonder what type of girl you were that could not get a man to marry her. You could be called names and, after a period of time, it would become more difficult for you to marry. 'If she is a good girl, why has she not married all this while?' men would ask. That was why many young girls did not wait to choose but jumped at the first available men who approached their parents. 'Marry and settle down,' the older women counselled us. 'Have your children and bring them up to serve you,' others said. 'May you prosper with your husband,' the family elders prayed.

"My man was young and handsome. I was his first and only wife; he had no concubine yet. That was the dream of us young girls at the time. We had seen our fathers with many wives and did not like the way our mothers were treated. We did not like the way our mothers lived, trying to out-rival one another at great costs to please one man who laid claim to all of them. The men were like kings and our mothers were their servers.

"I could not forget that I was the only child of my mother. She drummed it into my ears in different ways. Her encouragement to me was to have one child after another until my house was full. So I went into the marriage thinking that I would be pregnant from my first night. I had hitherto not known a man and passed the night in fear and prayers.

"Everything is in God's hand. I have come to believe more strongly in Him than ever. A woman who has only one child always wants him or her when grown-up to make up for the other children she couldn't bring from her own womb. My mother was waiting to see me pregnant. Six months of marriage passed without my becoming pregnant, then eventually two years.

"I had a standing invitation from my mother to come during my first pregnancy to deliver at home. At the time, expectant mothers did not go to maternities or clinics.

"Five years passed. When I visited my mother, I was asked many questions, most of them quite embarrassing. It seemed that my people believed that my husband didn't sleep with me. Can you imagine that? Our Ujevwe neighbours are very blunt: they call marriage 'sex partnership.' How could they ask whether my husband slept with me or not? Was he a eunuch perhaps? They even asked me that question! His own relatives must have said worse things about me. Being the woman expected to be pregnant, if my husband did his job, the rest was left to me. None of his relatives abused me directly. I nevertheless suspected that they blamed me for their son's childlessness.

Ten years passed. I went to masseurs and herbalists known to crack serious cases of barrenness. Desperation drives one to go to any length. How could I have submitted myself to the insults of many of those masseurs? They were more interested in sleeping with their patients than making them have babies with their husbands. My father did not show any signs of being worried. His other daughters were as prolific as dogs. My mother was noticeably agitated and grew moody because of me.

'Don't worry about me,' I told her.

'Why should I not be worried? A tree standing alone in a landscape is vulnerable from any storm,' she cryptically said.

'I know that. It is not our fault,' I explained.

'People are laughing. You don't hear what my mates say about you and me; if you did, you will be worried,' she revealed to me. Before now she had never ventured to tell me about what others thought about the two of us.

'I say, don't worry. I will have my children when *Osonobrughwe** wants me to. It's not just the time yet,' I said with some confidence.

'Better soon before you are menopaused. Have you ever

---

* Urhobo word for God

heard of a woman getting pregnant after being menopaused?' she asked me.

'No, but I am still young. I still have many years to bear ten children if that is what *Osonobrughwe* wants for me,' I said.

'How many years in a lifetime that you have to spend ten or twenty years of adulthood in a hut instead of a real home?' she asked.

"Her proverb was loaded. I loved my husband, but there are people not made to live together. We were not blessed with a child and because of this, we knew by the twelfth year that our marriage was doomed. We had tried every possible way to have a child but to no avail.

"I chose a good time to approach him to discuss what we should do, now that we had lost hope in our having a child together.

"Efecha was a good man and even though we would go our different ways, it was painful for both of us.

'My man, don't let this annoy you. You know a woman's time runs out fast. You know our customs. It's not that I don't want you, but I will want us to try ourselves elsewhere with other partners,' I begged him.

"He thought deeply. He must have faced the same dilemma without telling me. Our situation was not unique. There were precedents in Agbon of people separating for reasons of childlessness simply to re-marry and have children. Irede and Tega, for instance, are now both happy in their new marriages.

'It's neither your fault nor mine, I believe,' he told me. 'I can understand.'

'Don't be annoyed with me. I think our separation will be good for both of us,' I told him.

'We have to act before it is too late for either of us. This is like a boil which we have to cut - it will at first be painful, but in the end it will save us future pain,' he told me thoughtfully.

"No Agbon man would want to give up his wife to go and sleep with another man. And I knew it pained him. A brave man does not weep in public but instead at night in his bedroom. I believe he must have wept when he was alone.

"We did as our customs demanded for the dissolution of our marriage to make me free again. We informed our families about our decision. Before representatives of the two families, he released me from my oath to be faithful to him. He asked for and got back a token amount of money in place of the bride price he had paid for me to be his wife.

"When I arrived home, my mother wept. I had to console her.

'I am neither sick nor dead, why do you have to mourn?' I asked her.

'Yes, twelve years of marriage and still childless!' she intoned.

'Don't let that bother you. I will have my children at the right time,' I pleaded with her.

"It is always clumsy for a big woman to live with her parents. Such a situation puts the woman and her mother in an awkward position. A few times when men visited, the mother would feign she had something to do outside and leave her big daughter and her male visitor alone. But her doing so made me uncomfortable. After all, I was a full woman already and did not need to be shy before men. What does a cock skirt round a hen for other than to stir desire? Some men are scared from coming out openly to court a woman. But the brave and those really in love are not deterred by a market of eyes; rather, they are ready to cross seven rivers to meet you.

"A woman divorced, not for quarrelling with her husband or for any fault of hers or his, attracts many men. For reasons I cannot explain, I looked far younger than my age. I could compare favourably with many girls who were very grown-up before they married. My body was fresh, men told me; but I did not need to be told what they felt I would like to hear. I soon had many suitors.

"Freedom provides thrills and vexations. Half-men came, as well as full men. Poor and rich, handsome and ugly. My mother at first pretended as if she did not give birth to me from having a man, my father. She later told me that her house was like a market, to which came all kinds of men who sought me.

"You remember I told you of men who fear to come out or to say what they want. There were many of such. Those who will enter the storm to seize what they desire are few.

"Once Charles Itofe visited, I knew he would father my first child. He had gone through Standard Six before he started his own business in Okpara. He was a very neat man and everything he wore fitted him well.

"That's how I came to marry your father. In those days, big and experienced as I was, my bride price had to be paid before I stepped out to go to his house. Your father was not rich but was a very kind man. It is sometimes difficult to be kind and rich at the same time. Giving out what he worked hard for with both hands left no big fortune at home. A strong man, he impregnated me within three months.

"You can imagine my joy at being pregnant! With him what had been so difficult looked so simple. Then it was as if the moon shone continuously every night. I know that the patient fisher with God's help will always make a catch. I thanked God every day as I kept rubbing my swelling belly. I looked at myself in the mirror and danced naked in my room for joy. As if to gain for time lost, my belly was a huge calabash. My mother feared I might have twins, but I knew it was one. I didn't go to my mother; rather, we arranged for her to come to me after I had delivered.

"And you came to brighten my life with your first cry. Who says that motherhood is not enjoyable? It is true that I slept little the first three months of your childhood because you slept during the day and kept me awake at night. Despite that sleeplessness, I so much enjoyed my motherhood. I had been removed from the rumour list of barren women. I was now a mother. Your father and I were really happy and he was triumphant as if he had conquered the invincible. We were like young boys and girls never leaving each other. My mother joked that our love was stronger than *sosorobia*, that perfume that Gambari people sell or give in exchange for coral beads.

"But the twists and turns of my life were just beginning. I have not had the courage to tell you but I have to now. While you were still a suckling, only six months old, your father, that kind man, the man who took me out of childlessness, the man whose life blessed my life, suddenly collapsed and died. All you had been told was that your father died while you were young. I became widowed the first time at thirty.

"Who knows tomorrow? How could I tell that I, once childless in a twelve-year marriage, would suddenly become widowed after my first child? How could I foresee that I would be twice widowed and become a curse to many men? But what happens for the first time does not always start a trend.

"How was I going to mourn my Charles? Everybody told me to be strong to take care of you rather than make you an orphan. I was so distraught that people said I looked worse than a mad woman.

"I was asked to assist in washing his body. I felt it was cruel of his relatives to bring me face to face with the corpse of my dead husband at that time. They said it was the custom for the widow to perform some rites and I did them all, including having to take a sip of the water used in washing the body.

One could be misconstrued as not showing love for the deceased, if one refused to carry out what tradition prescribed. And I could be branded a witch if I didn't do the strange things they wanted done. I did my part to show gratitude and respect for your father.

"I worked hard as I mourned. You grew fast. Our people consoled me.

'Everything is in God's hands,' they said.

'Only God knows this,' others said.

"Kind words poured from family members. Elders softened the blow with proverbs. Soon I, who had almost killed myself by jumping into a well, saw cause to live. You were there for me.

'You have this fine boy to take care of,' some counselled.

'The stump will grow back into a tree,' others told me.

"Even before I had done a year of mourning, the Itofe family wanted to transfer me to some other man. Fortunately, your father was his father's only child and I refused to re-marry in the extended family. They said I must choose one of many men in the family and when they could not bend or break my resolve to be left alone, they asked me to choose you. I chose you as my *husband*, but everybody knew it was a meaningless gesture to keep myself free.

"Who says time does not heal wounds? It heals even the deepest of wounds. As you grew, I saw a plant out of the old stump. The elders are right, the stump of the *eke* tree is still the *eke* tree. You carry your father's birthmarks in two places.

"I remained in your father's compound. I had pressure from his family and mine to leave. Even friends asked why I should bite what I did not want to eat or swallow. Either I married from the Itofe family or left them and continued on with my life. Certain fires take a long time to cool. Such was the relationship between your father and me.

"You started elementary school. I was happy that the magic I was denied would now be exercised in my house. I was able to buy books and uniform for you without any problem. I did not mind that none of your father's relations, even those who wanted me as their wife, one day asked how you were being provided for. As you mature, you learn that everybody cares only for his or her own. Very few want to give out where they would not get back something. Since they could not have me, they abandoned me and mine, you. But the joy of your going to school invigorated me to work hard. My trade prospered. You were my *Obo* god, hence whatever I touched brought enough money for you and me to live on. I could raise my head high because I did not depend on any man who would ask me to do his bidding.

"When you were eight, I felt you needed a father. I also needed a man. I could not pretend that I was not a woman and so live alone the rest of my life. Men came to me again. They swarmed to me for attention. Some helped me clear my farm, others gave other types of assistance. I am a woman and after giving your father due respect, I threw away my rags. I chose Tebu who performed the customary demands of a would-be husband. He had divorced and I didn't really know why he did. However, I liked him and married again.

"It was as if a floodgate was opened. In five years I had three children, your two sisters and one brother. I thanked *Osonobrughwe* for the kindness. I went out to look for a worm and found a snake! Three other children surpassed my expectation. I gained weight from happiness and well-being. Tebu was happy, I was happy, you and the other children were happy.

"Then a storm struck from nowhere. That has always been my bane. Death visits when least expected. A healthy man went to bed at night and did not wake. That was how Tebu died. He was not sick of anything I knew of. He went to bed and the following morning when he did not respond to knocking on his door for so long, we had to break in to find his body already lifeless and stiff. You were already at St. Peter Clavers Grammar School at Aghalokpe then and came after your brother informed you of the bad news.

"Again widowed, I mourned. How could I take care of four children alone? My mother was dying herself, after she suddenly aged and I was alone like a water-lily shaking in the wide waters. I was bent on not getting torn off to drown. I did not need to be told. Men who married me who gave me love and children died suddenly. In Agbon bad things are said behind you. How was I not sure that they did not point fingers at me when I passed by them?

"I am not a witch, but I must be taken as one. I have heard of confessions of witches, I have heard of their flights to coven at night. They visit people with sicknesses or other problems in order to impoverish them. Women have been accused of killing their husbands. I did not make any effort to deny whatever the public chose to call me behind my back. I had no control over their imaginings.

"Again, I performed my rites when Tebu died. He was buried with a dog and I swore like his parents and close relatives that if anybody was responsible for his death, that person should fall sick and die. I was told that it was a trap they felt would catch me. My mind is as clean as *Orise*'s white chalk and I had no fears. My fear was for how I would take care of you all.

"I continued my farming and trading. Fortunately, after your early poor performance in college as a result of which I took you to my cousin in Jos, you changed to be so bright. I wanted you to be far from home so as not to be distracted by my mourning mood. You were already big enough to be troubled by my condition. With my mother dead, I had to think of dead husbands and a dead mother!

"With you away with my cousin who was then a major in the army, I set my mind on getting over my adversities. When you passed very well and got a scholarship for your university education, I poured libation on my *Obo* shrine. That was my way of thanking God on the good things I got despite the deaths surrounding me.

"For three years, I was like the *ogbo* charm tied to a fruiting tree. No man was bold enough to come close to me. No man appeared to want me and I wanted no man either. I was occupied with how to take care of my four children and that thought consumed all my time.

"More years passed. But soon, the fear that had kept men away appeared to be gone. They started to approach me, first indirectly and later directly. I was very surprised that men still wanted me. Men must be fearless or foolish because of women. If not, how could one explain their determination to have a woman like me as their wife or concubine? I would not allow my brother to go to a woman like me.

'Do you want to die?' I asked my suitors.

"After that blunt question, they did not return. They should have felt I was a witch or a crazy woman to ask them such a question. Human beings are fond of hiding their weaknesses or bad side. But I preferred to brandish the danger before those who wanted me. I would not, if at all I carried a jinx over my lovers, want anybody to die. Better warn them to run away.

"Thus, they flirted around me and whenever any came very close and expressed interest in a relationship, I drove them away with 'Do you want to die? Have you not heard that two husbands who gave me children died?' The chickens retreated and I didn't care about them. Those who had appeared very warm turned cold.

"Igbudu had lived among our people for so long that young Agbon people did not know he was not Urhobo. He has been accepted by our people as one of them. You know he is from Awka but speaks Urhobo more fluently than most of our *ototas*. He has been repairing bicycles in Okpara from my youth. He could forge iron into any farm tool. People loved him and he loved the town. I heard long ago that he had married, but the wife has since died.

"Igbudu was the only one not frightened by my question.

'Are you ready to die?' I asked him after he made known to me his proposal for us to be friends.

'Yes,' he-said. 'I know I will not; but if I have to die because of you, let it be,' he told me.

"I looked at him, from head to toe. He looked down on me because of his height. We gazed at each other for a long moment.

'Are you not afraid of dying?' I asked again.

'Your own people say that if you hear a gunshot, none should be afraid for the tortoise,' he told me.

'So you are the tortoise?' I asked.

'Yes, in a way. The hunter goes for grass-cutters, antelopes, porcupines and other animals but he never shoots at the tortoise,' he explained.

'You must be foolish to put yourself in the hunter's way and not fear being shot,' I told him.

'I am not afraid,' he insisted.

"I looked at him. I wondered whether he understood Urhobo ways enough, despite his long stay with us. He knew I was still worried about his daring proposal.

'Do you know I had lost a wife when I was much younger?' he asked me.

"I believe he felt it was his turn to frighten me out of a

close relationship now that he had declared that he cared more for me than for his own life.

'Yes, I know,' I answered him.

"I couldn't tell whether it was folly or courage, but there was love in our eyes. I knew he was serious about me.

'Come back to me when you are ready to die,' I told him.

'I am not going to think about it anymore. I have told you before and I want to tell you again that if I have to die for you, let it be,' he said so eloquently.

'If you are thinking right, why do you have to eat the very food that has killed others?' I asked him.

"I felt if he was not frightened stiff with this, then he should be a rare man. True to Igbudu, he did not waver.

'I am ready to die for marrying you. Nobody is going to live forever and whatever time I spend with you will be enough for me,' he said.

"My mind was made up. I would not give up the man who was ready to die for me.

'If I too have to die for you, I will,' I told him.

"He was greatly moved and sang one Urhobo song and an Ibo one for me. I cannot forget either of them. I had heard him before singing as he blew the bellows of his forge. Then he sang in a low tone as if coaxing the fire and his tools to do his bidding. Now his *Ubiebi fude, ubiebi fowe* made me young and excited again. I could only embrace him and we became husband and wife in everything but name. We were seen as concubines because we did not live under the same roof - he lived in his house and I lived in mine. I must say that marriage cannot be more delightful than what I have experienced with him. Igbudu gave me my last-born, Tietie. We have been together these past fifteen years. When he went to visit his people who were driven from the North, he was caught up with the war. I have not seen him for the past six months but I know he will cross the front-line of war to come back to me.

"I can tell you my son who will bury me that I have lived quite a life. Whether I recover or not, I have tasted the sweet and bitter draughts of life. There couldn't be more of life that I was denied."

That was how my mother, the great mother, my own *Ayayughe,* concluded her story. True to her prophecy, Igbudu came back, only too late. He arrived on the day the burial ceremony started. A man is not supposed to cry openly and profusely, but he did. Later he put the loss behind him and helped us in the burial, which I made as lavish and memorable as was possible. My mother would be proud of him as of us wherever she is now.

Death is such a depth that when I call, she cannot answer. Death is so severe that it cares not about those left behind. If death has not put such deaf distance between us, I would have liked to show her my gratitude for her love, care, and thoughtfulness. I remember when I failed my West African School Certificate examination and she took me to my cousin in Jos, Major Akoro. There they put me in a prep school and I had eight "A"s. I who had been dismissed as a dunce for failing every subject I wrote had become a wizard! All my brothers and sisters have been doing well at school and that has gladdened my mother's heart. She more than deserves the lavish burial we have given her.

the last-born

Titi and Mukoro Ubi, husband and wife, first met in the huge maternity ward of Warri General Hospital. That was sixteen years ago. Titi was then a Registered Nurse and had been enrolled in the Midwifery Programme to be a fully qualified and competent Nurse-Midwife in order to work with obstetricians in the Female/Maternity Ward. Apart from the high pay, being a nurse and a midwife gave you the necessary experience and confidence to work in the Female/Maternity Ward. If you were either a nurse or midwife alone, you were like a half-qualified person who sought advice for your missing knowledge. No wonder many female nurses who decided to specialize in female health liked to study midwifery. Titi had in her nursing school specialized in female health and surgery. Once she also qualified as a midwife, she knew the sky would be her limit in the profession. Titi spent the last three months of her Midwifery Programme in the same ward with Mukoro Ubi, MD.

The marriage of the nurse-midwife and the obstetrician was hailed as the God-made match. In Warri where there were many private hospitals and clinics, and one could not tell the difference from their names, most in the health and medical profession felt that the couple would start their own.

"They are sitting on a huge pot of fortune," other nurses and midwives said.

"They have made it," Dr. Ubi's colleagues said behind him.

"That man and woman would not smell want in their lives again," others said.

"God has blessed each with the other," some couples muttered.

"They will build their clinic and make millions of naira and live happily with their children," speculators said.

Conversations in Warri on whatever topic inevitably drifted to money. People came from different directions to make money in the oil city. In Warri, without money you were nothing. The rich were seen as naturally enjoying, and the poor suffering. A marriage that brought man and woman together to enhance their money-making capabilities was the ideal in the material view that pervaded the oil city.

Though the doctor and the nurse-midwife were drawn together the first time they met – an apparent case of love at first sight – Dr. Ubi was extraordinarily cautious. He was a professional and he knew, from his studies at the University of London and practice later at St. Mary's Hospital also in London, that the doctor should not involve himself romantically with his student training as a nurse-midwife. He knew too well how such relationships could go to brand one with irresponsibility in the public view, unless one covered up. To him therefore, those oaths of Hippocrates he swore to must now more than ever be upheld. In his white overall on top his suit, he projected himself as responsible and he did not want to soil his reputation. He felt that experience was one's best teacher.

So they played a cat-and-mouse game. They made sure they exchanged courtesies and looked beyond the wards for another kind of relationship, zealously guarding against being carried away by their feelings. Dr. Ubi had established himself here as an excellent obstetrician, trusted by pregnant women and their husbands. The chief rule in this profession is trust. If trusted, you would be sought wherever you were. And one had to be very good in one's job.

Dr. Ubi knew his job of delivering women of their babies very well. He could tell after an examination when labour would start and once it had started, he knew how long it would take before delivery. He had told women who said they were in labour to go home, that it was not yet labour. He was always borne out by the women's experiences. Before other doctors performed a caesarian section, they consulted him and he okayed it only if there was no other way for normal delivery. He knew a hopeless case when he met one.

Dr. Ubi felt he could operate a private clinic only after his retirement. He saw the conflict of interest involved in working for Warri General Hospital and for himself in his own clinic, though he knew other doctors did it. He was in a very small minority of doctors who did not have a private clinic or work after office hours for others. The job of a doctor was a twenty-four-hour commitment and there was no room for private practice, attractive monetarily as it was. A doctor must be ready at any time of the day or night to be called in case of an emergency and he stood ready. Most of the general practitioners referred people to their own clinics and their own drugstores. Dr. Ubi felt this practice was wrong.

Titi Toje in those days was a very determined woman. Her village of Utuyo was lost at the end of an impassable road. She had changed elementary schools, first attending St. Theresa's at Okpara Inland and then St. Charles' at Okurekpo. Even from her youth her fellow pupils and teachers saw in her a girl who carried her head high in the midst of boys. Her secondary education was the same, going first to Ughelli and then to Eku. She appeared to have stopped school suddenly or disappeared, only to reappear. Her visits to Utuyo to see her parents, brothers, and sisters were so infrequent that sometimes she did not appear there for two years. Many villagers felt she lived in Sokoto, Kano, or Maiduguri, distant places where many of their people had gone to work and make money.

But all the while, after her secondary education, Titi Toje was in Warri, the so-called oil city, to which people thronged from all corners of the Delta area. She remained invisible to her own people around her. She knew how to keep to herself, how in the crowd to be faceless.

The maternity ward in Warri General Hospital overflowed with babies. Dr. Mukoro Ubi joked that it seemed every love-making by Warri people resulted in a child. On a more scientific level, he felt there should be something in the fish and plantain that the people ate that made them very fertile. But he was not a biochemist to probe into that. As an obstetrician, he observed the phenomenon of high rate pregnancies. He was not surprised that the town was getting too crowded and the infrastructures could barely cope with the exploding population.

"Don't blame the people coming to work here; blame those who are already here who cannot control their appetites for making more children," he used to say.

As Warri General Hospital expanded with the baby boom that accompanied the prosperous oil decade of the 1970s, Dr. Ubi confined himself to the pre-natal clinic. "Catch the expectant mothers when there could be problems to save them from difficult deliveries" was his motto. He was still called for difficult deliveries, but his charge was the pre-natal ward.

Titi looked for ways to come and exchange greetings with Dr. Ubi, and if he did not see her before late afternoon, he strolled to the maternity ward to ask of her. There was barely a working day they did not see each other however fleetingly. That was after Titi completed her programme and started working full-time there.

The engagement a year after Titi completed her Midwifery Programme came as no surprise. Fellow workers praised Titi

Toje and Dr. Ubi for conducting themselves very well for so long. Many doctors openly went out with single nurses and midwives and saw that as part of what they jokingly called "bush allowance." Nevertheless, Dr. Ubi maintained his integrity where others brazenly immersed themselves in sexual frivolities. Titi and Mukoro expected their engagement from about the first time they met. It was the talk of the hospital.

The traditional marriage took place three months later, a few days before the church marriage. It was the first time Dr. Ubi saw Utuyo village. Before the traditional ceremony, Titi introduced her parents, brothers, and sisters to Dr. Ubi. Tetebe, the youngest girl, followed Titi everywhere she went. Their mother had to hold the little girl back to give Titi the chance to do what she had come for. Titi told Dr. Ubi how she was very fond of her youngest sister, Tetebe.

It was therefore natural that three months after the church marriage, Mrs. Titi Ubi had the following conversation with her husband.

"Mukoro dear, I'll like to bring one of my sisters, my mother's last-born, to live with us."

"What of her school?" he asked.

"She's still small and can go to any *akara* school here," she answered.

"That will be okay with me. Your mother needs some relief," the doctor told his wife.

"Thank you, dear. I know you will always support whatever will bring me happiness," she said as she embraced her husband.

"What is a husband for if he cannot reason with his wife and satisfy her simple demand?" Mukoro asked.

"You are a good man, that's why you say that. Not every man is as loving and kind as you are," she said smiling.

"And not every wife, love, is as loving and considerate as

you are," he said beaming with smiles.

They headed for the bedroom, after turning off the lights and the television. They had time together only at night as their days were mainly spent separately.

Titi decided to go home alone one Sunday to bring Tetebe. They returned so late that Dr. Mukoro Ubi had wondered why he did not accompany his wife to bring her sister. But as she had a good record of driving and her Beetle was serviced regularly, he was not too worried about her safety. He knew how in the village things went on a leisurely pace and one from the town could not hurry without being seen as rude and insulting. He remembered the traditional marriage ceremony during which it took hours to greet and be greeted by relatives close and distant, the prayers before breaking the kola-nut, prayers before serving the drinks, prayers and speeches that consumed time to no-one's concern. He imagined the elders praying for their daughter's well-being, which to them meant making babies and money.

Titi and Tetebe came back at night. There had been no problems at home.

"As you will expect, Tetebe was a little reluctant to leave but that was settled with my mother promising her impossible things," she explained.

"That's normal, dear," Mukoro replied.

"And with our big family, you can imagine the people who came in to be entertained under the pretext of coming to greet me," she added.

"I imagined that," he nodded.

It did not take Tetebe much time to adjust to the big house after leaving the one-bedroom home in the village. Her familiarity with Titi eased her transition and she made herself very comfortable.

"Sister, I need a new dress," Tetebe requested from Titi.

"Tetebe, you will get many good dresses," Titi assured her.

"When are you going to the market?" the young girl again asked.

"Don't worry. I go to the market any day I am off. Just be patient. Sister will buy you many clothes," Titi again assured.

"Sister, I did not bring my old clothes, the ones you bought for me last Christmas," the girl said.

Titi almost shut the girl's mouth with her palm. Her husband was busy in the bathroom and she felt spared being asked questions. After all, she had not told him that she bought clothes for her sisters at home during the Christmas.

Tetebe was like Titi's cat. She sat on Titi's lap even when she was with her husband and she would caress the young girl's hair. Titi took pains to plait Tetebe's hair herself on weekends. Tetebe freely entered the master-bedroom that Titi and her husband shared. Titi had a nominal room which she abandoned to Tetebe.

Tetebe looked every way well taken care of. She was healthy, buoyant, and neat. Titi and Mukoro provided for her as their own. Within a year of being with them, she had changed from a rather skinny child into a robust young girl. Both Mukoro and Titi were happy that she was happy living with them.

"Dear, you have made this possible," Titi told her husband.

"You are trying to be nice to me. It is you who made the suggestion and you should have the credit for Tetebe's well-being," he told his wife.

"Okay, we both wanted her with us and my mother should thank you in particular; after all, she's my sister," Titi said to please her husband.

"Every child's growth should be a thing of joy to us, more so somebody as close. Once we have a child, Tetebe will have a brother or sister here," Mukoro told her.

"When you are ready, I'll be ready," Titi said without shyness.

Both husband and wife knew what it would take for Titi to be pregnant. However, they wanted to show an example of planned parenthood, which Dr. Ubi taught women who came to his pre-natal clinic. For him, it meant a form of deliberateness which he had assumed in his life since he came back from London. Titi did not feel any hurry to have a child with him. After all, there was nobody saying that she was infertile and who has to be proved wrong. She was ready to wait, ready to enjoy herself, as she told herself, before carrying that nine-month handicap. From experience, she knew that men started to take you for granted after you have borne a child for them.

Two and a half years after their marriage, Titi became pregnant. Dr. Ubi said it was unprofessional for him to attend to his wife, and consequently she saw a different doctor. He mocked his wife and said that she was on trial. She delivered women of their babies and it was time for her to be delivered of her own baby!

"I will see how you will handle the pain for the first time," he told her.

"It doesn't matter whether it is the first, second, or last pregnancy, labour pains remain the same," Titi told him.

"You are both a nurse and a midwife and so should know better than me," he replied.

"You deliver babies too, so you should know how women in labour behave," she said.

"At the beginning, I almost couldn't bear the madhouse atmosphere but I got used to it," he said.

"It was the same for me as a nurse, I got used to their madness--some even tear off their clothes. But for the pregnant women, I don't think they ever get used to delivering. Each one appears to be a different painful experience," she told her man, speaking more as a woman than a nurse-midwife.

"I can understand," Dr. Ubi told Titi, "why women in the villages confessed any prior indiscretion they might have committed."

"It's a matter of life and death, dear. I wish men would experience it to understand why women in labour don't care whether they were stripped or not, why they broadcast every secret in their lives," Titi said.

"You can't change nature, dear. But do you believe if the women don't confess their misdeeds, anything would happen to them?" he asked.

"How can I believe that nonsense? Men do worse things than women and are never put in a position to confess their own misdeeds. Those women who confess are cowards. It is superstitious to think that you can't deliver because another man touched you. It is simply a matter of guilty conscience. Those who are guilty always suffer, whether at delivery or at other times," she told her husband.

Dr. Ubi was touched by Titi's passion on the issue of labour. As an obstetrician, he was supposed to ease the fears of pregnant women and he found himself in an uncomfortable position appearing to scare his own pregnant wife. From his experience so far, Titi was not a woman who would be scared.

Titi Ubi went to work during her pregnancy and continued to deliver women. She now chastised younger nurses or midwives who made fun of women in labour, teasing them with statements such as these:

"I de there when you de do am?"

"Why you de cry when you enjoy am when you de do am?"

"If the thing pain you, no do am again."

When her time came, Titi was put in a private room to experience what the women she had been administering to went through. She was anxious, since she believed that no matter how many times a woman had delivered, every delivery was painful. She also believed that no amount of experience in delivering others absolved one from anxious sweat. However, everything went smoothly. Titi delivered a girl, whom she and her husband named Eloho. Titi and Dr. Ubi were elated to have their own child.

As Eloho grew, she began to call Titi "Mummy." Of course, Eloho was like a junior sister to Tetebe. A certain rivalry often arose between Tetebe and Eloho, which Mukoro and Titi observed.

"Don't mind her, she is jealous of Eloho," Titi told Mukoro of Tetebe.

"It's natural for a child to feel that way," Mukoro responded.

"I didn't know jealousy could begin so early," she admitted to her husband.

"You know the way brothers and sisters are jealous of the last-born in the family, so Tetebe is jealous of the young one who draws almost all of the attention from her," he explained.

As husband and wife sat to relax after the evening meal, the two children came to them pushing each other.

"Why can't I call you Mummy too?" Tetebe asked.

"Yes, call me Mummy. I am your Mummy too," Titi answered her.

"And you Daddy," Tetebe told Dr. Ubi.

"Yes, you are my daughter and I am your Daddy," he assured her.

Anybody who saw Tetebe and Eloho would take them as sisters, the same glowing dark complexion, the same half-parted lips, the same long eyelashes.

"You and your mother have delivered sisters," Mukoro Ubi told his wife.

"Of course, the fruit of one tree will sprout to grow the same tree. After all, the same genes passed from my mother to me and my sister and from me to Eloho," Titi said, as if in self-defence.

Titi did not relate differently to both Tetebe and Eloho. However, Tetebe was not as close to Mukoro Ubi as Eloho was.

Dr. Ubi was appointed Chief Medical Director of the Warri General Hospital. His promotion was an elevation his rivals conceded he more than deserved. He acquired more responsibilities that required more energy and time to reorganise a hospital which he believed he could operate more efficiently. At a meeting of all the hospital workers, he made his priorities known:

"It is true we have a government budget every year. From now on, however, we have to make money to subsidize what the government gives us. You all know things will be better for each of us if we have more money to improve the different wards and to help our workers in many ways. Salaries alone are not enough for workers. Having a restaurant whose good meals are subsidized will benefit everybody. Having a club where workers can bring their family members to relax after work and on weekends will ease much of the stress which goes with the type of work we do," he told his co-workers.

He inspired his fellow doctors to behave with propriety; patients could tell that there was a change in the general atmosphere of the hospital. The place was swept regularly and doctors and nurses who used to wear slippers to work stopped doing so and began wearing court shoes instead. Dr. Ubi wanted to make a difference and he succeeded within a short time to give a good face to Warri General Hospital. It was no longer seen as the dump of the poor but as a place where doctors, nurses, midwives and other support staff were very professional in their work.

While Titi worked in the morning shift, Dr. Ubi was in and out of shifts, in addition to his regular morning one. The plan for his personal clinic was delayed because of his new appointment. He said he could not be an effective boss in two different capacities, at Warri General Hospital and in his private clinic. One had to give way to the other.

Dr. Ubi now worked until late. He had to make sure that there were enough doctors on call. In addition, he had to go the rounds of wards to see things for himself. When he came home late, he tried his best to relax with his wife. He often teased her.

"You have converted me to a night bird," he told her.

"I hope you don't mean you are a wizard, an owl?" Titi asked.

"You know what I mean," he replied.

"Why are you a night bird?" she queried, waiting for him to explain.

"You remember you only wanted us to make love at night? Now I wouldn't have time during the day even if you were to change your time," he told her.

"I believe sex is meant for the night," she said.

"Where did you read or hear about that?" he asked.

"This has nothing to do with reading or hearing from somebody else. It is what I think is convenient. How could I be struggling with both Eloho and Tetebe during the day and still have time to be relaxed enough to be with you?"

"Okay, you are right. I don't think so, but I will do what pleases you, my sweet and tough Titi," he said tenderly.

From the beginning of their intimacy, Titi formed the habit of switching off the lights before love-making. According to her, light distracted her from giving her full self to what she would be doing. She also remained half-dressed, always in her bras.

"Shy woman, when will you strip for me in light?" Mukoro asked her.

"What do you want to see in me that you have not yet seen? Are you not an obstetrician, or are you a priest?" she asked.

"I want to see how you respond to me sometimes," he said.

"Don't you enjoy me enough all these years?" she asked.

"I didn't say so," he replied.

"Then why do you want a change?"

"Just for the sake of change, for variety."

"If you want variety that much, I hope you will not go and sleep with another woman," suggested Titi.

"Of course, I won't. You know I won't do that," he protested.

"What prevents you when you want variety? You say you don't like our traditional people, but you want what they want. They claim that one woman kills a man's desire," she said jokingly.

"You know that you always make me hungry for more of you," he said.

"You have not said that before now. Why are you saying that today?" she asked.

"Okay, that's enough. We shouldn't be talking this way," he told her.

Mukoro never wanted to hurt his wife and he felt she was not pleased with the exchange. He was teasing her and did not want what should have been a joke to bring a quarrel between them.

By the fourth year of their marriage, Titi was pregnant again. They had planned to space out their children to provide an example to other women who were breeding children like chickens. It told on the woman, Dr. Ubi had been saying. Titi had also been telling her patients that she could have a child almost yearly if she chose to but she wanted herself and her babies to be healthy. Many of the women said it was not up to them, that their counselors should talk to their husbands.

"But it is your body," Dr. Ubi would tell them.

"Go and say that to my husband," a pregnant woman told him.

"Bring him here and I will talk to him," he advised.

"Have you seen an Urhobo man near where his wife is delivering?" she asked.

"He doesn't need to be physically by your side to understand what you go through," he told the expectant mother.

"Are you Urhobo or Ibo?" the woman asked.

"It doesn't matter who I am, I am human," he answered.

Dr. Ubi started a counseling clinic for women who have delivered more than three children and whom he wanted to make understand that each additional pregnancy imperiled their health. The younger women were able to bring their husbands and many agreed with Dr. Ubi's prescription of just having a few children.

Titi delivered a boy and she was happy that she now had male and female children. They named him Tega. The baby boy grew fast and soon became a warrior in the house, fighting with the two girls far bigger than him. He stopped his warrior-like attacks after Tetebe one day gave him serious beating. Dr. Ubi was annoyed that such a grownup girl who should have sense of right and wrong would physically beat a toddler.

"Don't do that again," he warned Tetebe. "What if Mummy and I were out and only three of you were home, do you mean to tell me that this is how you would be beating your small brother?" he asked.

"He scratched me and would not stop, he is always looking for our trouble," Tetebe explained.

She promised not to beat the boy again. But even the boy started to fear the girls as he felt they would always strike him back more harshly than he did to them.

After three years, Dr. Mukoro Ubi asked Titi to stop taking pills and be ready for another child.

"Better have all three children we want before we get old," he suggested to her.

"That's fine with me," she answered.

Then started a period in which the nurse-midwife and doctor started to doubt their own fertility and virility respectively. Three years passed, and still no pregnancy. Titi was now in her mid-thirties. As a midwife, she knew that delivery became more difficult as women aged. She was ready to be pregnant to have yet another child but things could not work well. Though they had planned for three, they felt blessed with the two children that they already had together.

Dr. Ubi didn't visit home with his wife and children. He was more of a townsman. The very little time he had he occasionally spent at the Warri Club where the successful professionals wined and dined. He was a teetotaller and he drank only club soda. Some of his colleagues in the club teased him that he would live forever and inherit the earth. But he was not moved by taunts to do what his profession knew was bad to one's health, taking alcohol. His people did not visit him, nor were there people he could call friends who visited him. Titi and Dr. Ubi were each other's friend, brother and sister.

Time passed quickly. The Ubis celebrated their tenth marriage anniversary at home. The celebrants did not invite anybody from outside. Rather it was a feast for man and woman with their two children and Tetebe. By the time they celebrated their fifteenth marriage anniversary, Tetebe had finished secondary school and entered the University of Benin to study Psychology and Drama. Both Mukoro and Titi wanted to steer her to study any of the sciences, but she said she wanted to have a combined honours degree so as to be very marketable when she finished her programme. They could not persuade her to change her course of study.

By Tetebe's final year at the University of Benin, she was big enough to bring a young man home to tell the Ubis about their intention to marry. The young man who was working at the Nigerian Television Authority in Benin was anxious to meet her people, especially her parents, and arrange for the traditional marriage before Tetebe graduated and a church wedding would take place. Better to rein the young women before they went on national service and some rich *alhajis* spoilt them!

David Ode was directed to Utuyo village to see Tetebe's father. There Titi's mother and father entertained the young man and then together with some old family members left the main house to consult far from their visitor's ears. They came back and Titi's father cleared his throat.

"My son, we are happy that you like our daughter and want to marry her. Once a woman grows up, she has to marry. That's our custom. We men also have to marry. Tetebe has gone to the university and we are happy. We want the man who is marrying our daughter to be our son. You will be our son," he told David Ode.

Tetebe had gone to meet the women who were celebrating her visit. It had been some years since she came to Utuyo.

"Utuyo's soil will bless you, David. We agree for you to marry Tetebe. We will also want you to go to Sapele to see her junior father," he told Mr. Ode.

That was how David Ode went to Sapele to see the man who fathered Tetebe. He was a Senior Clerical Officer at the African Timber and Plywood Company, a subsidiary of UAC, the multinational conglomerate in colonial and contemporary Africa.

Mr. Kurusu had been introduced to Tetebe in one of his

rare visits to the Ubis as her cousin. He was lavish in the money he left for Tetebe. Titi often talked about him to Tetebe as he continued to send the girl pocket money through her. Nobody would see anything unusual in a working cousin assisting a young lady in school and whose father was a village farmer.

Though not a socializer and mixer, whisperings of Tetebe's parenthood finally reached Dr. Ubi. Most of his colleagues heard of it, kept mute and waited for an opportunity to shock him. Soon it was public information of the senior workers of Warri General Hospital. They talked openly about it and whenever either Titi or Dr. Ubi appeared, they changed to some unrelated topic. But, as they say in Warri, do-gooders are many. They are always waiting to steal into you while alone and volunteer to tell you what everybody else but you know. Senior Nurse Tricia was one of Dr. Ubi's trusted workers who entered his office without restriction.

"Sorry-o Doctor, this thing about Tetebe being Madam's own daughter na-waoo!" she said as if Dr. Ubi was already aware of what she was revealing.

"Beg your pardon, you say what?" he asked.

"I hear say Tetebe no be Madam sister but na in daughter," she explained.

Dr. Ubi always comported himself, but more so while at work. He was stunned by what he was hearing, but he had to appear unruffled.

"I hope you no go vex with Madam, na so we women be," Senior Nurse Tricia pleaded.

"Women and men are the same," he told her.

By the time Tricia left his office, Dr. Ubi had obtained a lot of information. He wondered how others were able to know so much while he was in the dark. He felt stupid and naive that he did not know Tetebe was not really his wife's sister. After more people told him what they heard, he was in the greatest dilemma of his life.

The story he reconstructed was that Mr. George Kurusu, then in Class V, impregnated Titi who was then in Class IV. That led to her withdrawal from St. Theresa's Grammar School, Ughelli, for a year. After her delivery of Tetebe, she transferred the following year to Baptist High School, Eku.

"Is she really your daughter?" he asked his wife later on getting home in a tone that was neither of anger nor of tenderness.

There was something in his voice which was strange to her and Titi felt cornered.

"Why do you ask?" she countered.

"I want to know, hear the facts from your own mouth," he answered.

"What facts do you want from me? She calls me Mummy and what else do you expect of her and me?" she retorted.

Titi, without saying it all, defiantly confirmed that she and her townsman, Mr. George Kurusu, parented Tetebe. Her mind went back to the afternoon "jump" at Joint One in Enerhe Road by Warri-Sapele Road. They left the dance and headed straight for Kurusu's rented room and the rest of that afternoon was the fact of Tetebe.

Dr. Ubi felt so bad about his stupidity of being an obstetrician and not knowing that Titi had borne a child before their marriage. He could recollect clearly Titi's saying in their days of courtship that he should not expect a virgin of her.

"Who needs a virgin these days?" he had asked in order to show that he didn't care about what he termed an obsolete virtue.

Now he could tie a lot of things together. Titi had remained shy for all the seventeen years they had been husband

and wife. No wonder she half-covered herself even at most intimate moments. Dr. Ubi remembered their church marriage seventeen years earlier and the priest reading what he felt then was ominous. It was a charge:

"I require and charge you both,...if either of you know of any impediment, why you may not be lawfully joined together in matrimony, you do now confess it. For be well assured that all those that are coupled together *otherwise* than as God's word allows, are not united by the Lord."

He noticed the faltering voice of Titi as she repeated her response to the charge before him, the priest and the congregation.

"I solemnly declare that I know not of any lawful impediment why I, Titi Toje, may not be joined in matrimony to Mukoro Ubi."

It was after both had made their similar responses that the priest pronounced, "What God has joined together, let no man put asunder."

At first Dr. Ubi felt betrayed and angry, but more with his own stupidity at being so easily deceived for so long than with Titi. What was he to do? He dismissed the so many vengeful thoughts that came to his mind as puerile and devilish. Their marriage had been good and happy, no matter the foundation of deceit that it was built on. He remembered *Even God Is Not Ripe Enough*, a tale on how a determined woman was able to deceive God. Though he would not go the male chauvinist way, he saw that women before marriage like men could cover up for their own interests. He told Titi in the morning as he went to work that they would have a chat at night.

Titi was anxious but calm like a person in the river, knowing she could not fall below the river's bed. She would explain why she had to keep the secret for so long from him. She had many fears and had thought he knew from the way

Tetebe and herself related. She would not excuse herself for not telling him from the beginning of their courtship, but would apologise. Once she didn't tell him before or after the bride-price paying ceremony, it became more difficult afterwards. By the time she brought in Tetebe as her sister, her mother's last-born, the matter had grown beyond what she could reveal without damaging their marriage. She was wrong, but with reasons.

That night Titi prepared Mukoro's favourite meal to soften what she expected would be his disappointment with her and perhaps the end of their marriage. Mukoro ate the dodo and rice with fresh fish with a lot of relish. Then they left the dining table for their bedroom where there was a comfortable lazy-boy, "me-and-my-partner." Titi's heart beat fast and her breathing was loud. She did not know what to expect.

"I want us to resolve this matter once and for all and put it behind us," Dr. Ubi said.

Titi's heart still beat fast but her breathing came back to near normal. Before she could think of what to say, Mukoro continued. He said he was going to make a confession of his own. He told how during his medical training in London he had married Tilly, a rich white lady much older than him but that the marriage broke down just before he flew back to Nigeria. Since his arrival and up to that day, he had never heard of Tilly again but their marriage was never officially dissolved.

"I assume Tilly should either have remarried or taken a boyfriend. She was a nurse at the hospital where I did my housemanship," he told Titi.

Titi had regained her normal heartbeat and breath. She expected an assault but met a retreat. What else could she say? Mukoro told Titi that the revelation that she had Tetebe before their marriage was understandable and the whole matter

was a storm in the tea-pot. He set a date for his early
retirement so as to start their own clinic. It had taken them
almost twenty years to do what they should have done from
the beginning. Titi said she would also retire at the same time:
in six months.

With the lights still on, Titi undressed and threw bra and
night dress on the floor and smiling and holding Mukoro to
herself, whispered into his ears "Here I am for you."

my master's son-in-law

I did not know my own parents and the brothers and sisters I might have. Vera and I grew up together in their home. I knew from the beginning that Mr. Tadafe was not my father, nor Madam my mother. They treated me as one of them, but there was a difference. I was brought to help Madam and her children with household chores.

I slept alone in the boy's quarters, which consisted of two one-room apartments, about twenty yards to the back-side of the main house. The other room was unoccupied and empty. Most of the time I could not hear or see what was happening in the main house. However, when they shouted for me, I could hear. When they beckoned on me to come, I could see them. I liked my six-spring bed and I had become used to sleeping alone. At night I listened to the crickets chirruping, owls hooting, and other creatures that must be enjoying the night. If they did not enjoy the night, they would have kept quiet like me.

When I woke in the morning, I looked forward to the big clock in the house to strike six times. Because it was cool and quiet in the morning, the six strokes sounded louder than they did during the day. Many afternoons, I did not hear the clock strike but the morning strikes served me well. Once I heard the final of the six strokes, I got up and went to sweep the sitting room. After sweeping the floors, I helped to bathe Tejiri who was of about the same size as me. Madam bathed Vera after I was done with Tejiri.

I would not say that I was overworked. No, Madam did

some work too. She did the cooking and might once in a while ask me to wash plates. I think Mr. Tadafe liked his plates very clean and Madam would not offend him by making me wash them. I had witnessed them exchange words only once. That was over the glass of water which had some dirt in it.

"This boy didn't wash the glasses clean," Madam told him.

"Don't give me any excuse," he shouted.

"I am not giving any excuse, he washed the glasses and plates," Madam explained.

"I don't want to drink with a dirty glass again. If it was the boy who washed the glasses and plates, know that it is your duty as my wife to give me clean glasses and water. If I fall sick, I hope you will not blame the innocent boy," he told her.

From then on, Madam relieved me of washing plates and glasses; in fact, of everything used in serving Mr. Tadafe at table.

When guests came, I was sent to bring out or buy drinks, cigarettes, and kolanuts. Whether I was given money or not, the sellers knew Mr. Tadafe very well and would give whatever he had asked for. They knew he would pay them however much they said he was owing them. I served the drinks very well and got praised. I mastered easily the art because it did not require extraordinary skill to serve the local gin. I held the bottle with the left hand and, slanting it at a certain angle, poured it into a small glass in my right hand. Serving beer was even easier. I poured it gently and in drips so that the beer glass filled without any foam. I made a mistake the first time by filling the glass with foam which overspilled and ruined the table cloth but I learnt my lesson and never made the same mistake again. Though I served Mr. Tadafe's guests with local gin, beer, and cigarettes, I never tasted any of them.

I served everybody in the house. Sometimes, it seemed as if I were not one person, since they wanted me for different things at the same time. Somehow I coped with the different demands, especially those of Daddy. We all called him Daddy, but I did not call Madam Mummy as Vera and Tejiri did.

Daddy always praised me for my work. He usually talked of how young I was and yet how careful I had already become.

"Keep your good behaviour up and you will grow into a successful man," he said.

I redoubled my effort the more to be a good boy and to become a successful man when I grew up. If Daddy wished me well as he always did, I knew that I had to continue working hard and behaving well to become a big man like him.

He was a cheerful, happy, and generous man. He observed my low mood and cast jokes to make me laugh and forget about my thoughts. He generously gave out with both hands to his relatives who visited often. He gave me pocket money and told me to always remind him of whatever I wanted. He bought clothes for me as he did for his two children. Tejiri and I were of the same age, maybe I was six months older than him. Vera was three years younger than me. She was two when I came to the house.

Mr. Tadafe praised me before all his guests, relatives and friends.

"This is an intelligent boy and I won't like him go to waste," he told his good friend Mr. Ubogun, who visited him often.

"What do you want to do for him, other than his living with you now?" Mr. Ubogun asked.

"Send him to school," Daddy told him categorically.

"If you have to, better now before he gets too big," Mr. Ubogun suggested.

"In fact, I have made up my mind about his going to school with Tejiri next year," he confided in Mr. Ubogun.

That was how I went to elementary school with Tejiri,

ahead of Vera. By the time Tejiri and I were in Primary Six, Vera was in Primary Three. I took the first position in my class, Tejiri took the second position. Daddy was happy that I performed so well. Madam did not quite show her happiness openly. The vacation that followed the school year was a sad one for all of us.

Without any warning, we lost Tejiri. He had gone out to play and a passing car struck him and sped away. Daddy was not at home. Before Madam could get him to hospital, he had died. I will never forget the cold in the house for the next three months. When somebody dies newly, the person still lives before those who had been close to him or her. We felt Tejiri was there, but the space was empty. We felt stared at by the invisible eyes of the deceased.

Many visitors came to console Daddy and Madam. At the beginning they sat for a long time to condole Tejiri's father and mother. I heard some of them saying that if it was not God's will, Tejiri would not have died. Then and now I don't know whether God loves or hates the dead. But I agree it must be God's will to be knocked dead by a passing car that could not be identified.

Nobody cared about Vera and me who were closest to Tejiri. Children were not supposed to feel a loss. Children were not supposed to be consoled. Every adult who paid a condolence visit must have felt that children did not understand what death meant and so had no need to be talked to. Nobody knew our fears. I was afraid because I saw his dead body and was always thinking that he might come back to life at night to take me to the world of death. I knew that Vera also felt Tejiri's loss deeply as she became very cold. The talkative person I was growing up with became taciturn and only talked sparingly when talked to. I knew she might have felt like me, especially at night, that Tejiri would visit her and she would be dead. As time went on, my fear wore off. I believe Vera's too waned.

I had been teaching Vera after school before Tejiri died. After the loss of her brother, she came even more to me with her homework. Daddy could help but the assignments were simple enough for me to assist without his involvement. She was very inquisitive and asked many questions. I could not answer all of her questions but I tried my best.

"Why does the goat walk on four legs instead of on two?"

"Why do we have to boil yam before eating it?"

"Why is Daddy not pregnant?"

"Where is God?"

"Will Tejiri come back?"

I helped her more, solving the Arithmetic and Civics questions, which needed right or wrong answers than in providing solutions to the general questions. Even later when I was grown up and we had become even closer than when children, I teased her saying that I couldn't still answer those questions that popped out of her head, rather than came out of her books. She couldn't even remember that she had asked me such questions. Then and much later she remained the same lively person.

I will always be grateful to Vera's father, my master, for sending me to school. He treated me as his own and I had no problem with school uniform and textbooks. He was very pleased with my constant first position from Primary One to Six.

I passed the entrance examination to Federal Government College, Sokoto. Vera's father was reluctant to send me to what his friends called the end of the world. But he had always been a very considerate man and he knew I would like being a pioneer student of the Federal Government College, Sokoto, one of only three Unity Colleges nationwide. That was in 1966 the year of the first military coup in Nigeria. The nation was shaky but the security arrangements and assurances made for us convinced Daddy to release me. He accompanied me in the Armels Transport lorry to Oshogbo where I took a train to Gusau where the college driver came to pick us.

I won a scholarship at the end of the first term when I took the first position in my class. I maintained my first position and my studies from then till now have been sponsored by one Federal or state scholarship after another.

During holidays I went back to Vera's father's, my home. I missed Tejiri. We might have been in the same Federal Government College and he would have remained a good companion. But I had to go alone to college where both of us would have gone to study at the same time.

I still retained my boy's quarters. Daddy and Madam got another house help, a girl from Calabar, who slept in the other room next to mine. She had more assignments than I ever had. She got paid every month and I knew neither how she saved her money nor what she did with it. However, I did not allow college to get into my head to the extent of forgetting that I came in as Daddy's house-boy. I wanted to sweep and clean the house, wash clothes, but Vera's father without asking me to stop told me to read rather than work.

"If I wanted you to continue doing this work, I wouldn't have sent you to school in the first place," he told me.

"Thank you. I will work a little and read more of the time," I replied.

Even then I knew I was paying back for the kindness he had done for me. I really did not work much during vacations as I was busy with my own reading or helping Vera with her homework and later her preparations for the common entrance examination which she would take in two years. Daddy and Madam encouraged her to bring her books to me in the boy's quarters. From their interest in me there was no doubt that they wanted some of my Federal Government College experience to rub off on their daughter.

When I was twelve, Vera was nine. I told her about the train journey. I described the rhythmic throttling noise. The spectacle of trees and buildings seemingly racing past the train, when in fact it was the other way around. The hornblast before a station to forewarn passengers to get ready to disembark or embark. The station master's whistle. The beggars who travelled free stretching pans before you to drop them coins. The savannah stretch of plains. Cotton and groundnut pyramids. Guinea fowl eggs. Corn. Pretty Fulani girls and women selling *fura de nono*, with calabashes of milk balanced on their coiffurred heads.

"I also want to go to your Federal Government College," Vera told me as she heard the story of my train trip to school.

"You are on your way there already," I told her.

"How?" she asked.

"By reading for the common entrance examination," I explained.

"If I don't go to Federal Government College, I won't go to any other school," she promised.

Vera passed the entrance to the Federal Government Colleges but was placed in Warri. We had visited the college and she had been impressed by the smart students in their white-and-green uniform, the vast, neat and well laid out compound, and an atmosphere of freshness bubbling with excitement. She was elated that she was admitted into this Federal Government College and did not regret not being sent to Sokoto.

"We will compare our experiences," she told me.

"Better that we have to tell each other different things. You will then be teaching me something and I will be teaching you something new," I said.

"Won't that be great, exchanging ideas on our two great Federal Government Colleges?" she asked.

"I can't wait for the next Christmas holiday when we will be home together," I answered.

We separated during school time. We wrote each other letters, each praising his or her school. On holidays we met. At such times, Vera did most of the chores assigned to me. The girl from Calabar was gone, according to Madam, to marry at that young age rather than go to school. Since we were the only two children in the house and being students of Federal Government Colleges, we were always by each other.

Both of us did well in the West African School Certificate examination. I made seven As and Vera would later make six As. I was far in the medical school at the University Teaching Hospital, Ibadan, when Vera entered the University of Ibadan to read English and French. She wanted to work either in the foreign service or as an interpreter in a multi-national company.

We travelled together from home, visited each other every weekend at Ibadan no matter how busy we were. I did not waste time to send for her from the Queen's Hall porters as she was always around expecting me about the late morning of Saturdays when I called. She came to the Medical Students' Hall in Bodija quarter of Ibadan after service on Sunday.

Both of us were growing big. We knew what other male and female students were doing. They went to parties together, they slept together. We were no longer innocent though we did not do what we knew others were doing. I thought of Vera often. She bought presents for me and I reciprocated. We became inseparable, especially on weekends. We were reluctant to leave each other. Our touch became warmer and more tender. I was confused about her and she also appeared confused about me. We looked at each other longingly, reluctant to break hold of each other.

It was in a letter that she wrote "I love you," and I wrote back "I love you too." When we met after this declaration, we knew there would be a world of experience for us to explore in our hunger and desire for each other. Our hearts beat for each other and we longed for each other's body. All of a sudden, it was as if there was something running from one body to the other when I held her hands. She never took her hands away from me. When we kissed in my room, we knew it was a matter of time before we went to bed.

We were free at Ibadan but we knew that one's well-being rested in the other's and as such had to be restrained. How many times we embraced, held each other tight, kissed, and sighed for what we could get away with but denied ourselves to stay close. Vera understood how her parents would feel, more so as she was still in school. Many times Madam had told her sometimes to my hearing that one did not hurry to where one would pass the night or sleep. In other words, she would marry but it was necessary for her to get her degree and be mature enough to do what pleased her. I did not know why both Daddy and Madam felt I must be some saint who was not interested in girls generally and certainly not in Vera, though my entire body burned with desire for her. How could they know that their servant though grownup could have feelings that are natural to a young man for their own daughter?

I had finished my housemanship when Vera graduated with a second class upper division. She was beautiful, slim, and agile. She exuded confidence in whatever she did--in her conversations, in her studies, and in her works. She glowed in her cheerfulness. She tried to involve me in whatever she wanted to do and I did the same. Our birthdays were mostly celebrated by both of us. I remember Vera's refusal to go home for her eighteenth birthday, though specially invited by her mother. She asked Madam to mail her birthday card and gift because she wanted to be with me. She felt it would raise alarm if both of us went home for the birthday celebration.

But the alarm she feared soon struck. There are certain things you cannot hide, or which you try to hide but not for too long. Love is one such thing. Its scent is stronger than designer perfumes. You couldn't be in love and not be known. Love gave us out with time, no doubt. It was when we were already big that Daddy and Madam started to be alarmed about our closeness. Finally, as adults they soon realized that we were in love with each other, but this was already late in our relationship.

Love made me to know myself. Daddy and Madam were hard but were not mean. Daddy was very subtle in telling us to look for other partners.

"You are both my children and I won't like this to happen," he counselled.

He felt we should understand what he meant, and we understood very well his cryptic but clear language.

"There are many young girls outside for you to choose from," Madam told me as if Vera did not have many young men to choose from too.

"With time both of you will forget about each other once you start to work in different places," Daddy said.

Both Vera and I sat and listened, without talking. We wanted to be polite and not interrupt Daddy or Madam. They suspected that their advice would not separate us.

"All I am saying," Daddy said, "is that I don't think both of you are making the best decision in going out together. You might be better off remaining as brother and sister," he said.

He kept quiet for some minutes, an interval in which we all looked at each other attempting to read the other's mind.

"I have no problem, but know that we want the best for both of you," Daddy concluded.

This was encouraging and it made Vera and me feel as if a heavy load had been taken off our backs. I knew Mr. Tadafe was my benefactor and I should not cut off the hand that had fed me from childhood into manhood. I was already a medical doctor working at Warri General Hospital but I continued to treat Mr. Tadafe with the respect reserved for a father. We wanted to get his permission however grudgingly for Vera and me to get engaged and to marry. And when we knew he had softened, indirectly granting us permission to do what we wanted, we were very happy.

But that was not the end of the resistance to Vera and me marrying. Soon his relatives hectored them to stop our plan. When they knew he would not go back on his tacit approval of our marriage, they came out openly to quarrel with him and humiliate me before Vera.

A family delegation of two men and one woman came from his Agbon home to see him and warn me, as they put it, from tainting their daughter. Daddy called me and I went, unaware of his town's people's mission to be very brazen in their insults so as to separate Vera and me.

"What's your name?" Osiebe asked me.

"Isaac Oghuvwu," I answered.

"I told you," Osiebe told his delegation with a mischievous smile.

"You think I don't know that your great-great-grandfather was a slave?" Osiebe asked me.

Being Daddy's brother, he felt he could say whatever he liked. Daddy was visibly angry and used his right hand to press me down. He felt I was going to walk out. I would not because of him.

"And then when your great grandfather owed and could

not pay back, you know what happened?"

"Brother, you don't need to ask Isaac this type of questions. He is a small boy, even though a medical doctor," Daddy answered for me.

"Let me tell him. Aje, Olotu's son, ordered his corpse to be brought to his compound and challenged your family to redeem the body or he would have it buried in his own bush. The puncheon of palmoil or the money equivalent was not paid because everybody in the family was poor, and Aje buried the body in the bush where none of your family up till today knows. Your men and their wives ran out of Agbon, went to Ulaje and Oshogbo areas in Yorubaland to fish or farm because they no longer dared show their faces in town. Your parents left you and have not visited for one day ever since. We tell you that they are dead but nobody really knows or cares about their whereabouts. You cannot marry our daughter," he said, exhausted.

I don't know why Mr. Tadafe allowed him to complete the insult. He might himself be hearing this for the first time, but he and Madam were enraged.

"It's your daughter. Let her marry into a slave family. If she does, you will no longer be one of our own freeborn," Osiebe said and spat out from his seat.

Mr. Tadafe had had enough. Brother or not, there was no reason for Osiebe to be rude to him in his own house.

"Leave my house and don't you ever come here again. This young man is a human being and if he and Vera love each other, they will marry despite his background. You would not see him to insult if I did not ask him to come," Daddy said passionately.

"We knew all along that you are lost. We are not surprised," Osiebe said as he left the house.

How could I at twenty-seven know that a hundred years

earlier lived a bonded man who was to give birth to three generations of which I am now the carrier of their stigma? But I was not hurt. Daddy and Madam forbade them from entering their home again because of their wounding revelation. I don't know whether they knew or not, but they wanted to shield me from being hurt.

Vera's family was from the freeborn tree, mine from descendants of truce guarantors. We were not slaves as such because our foreparents were brought to Agbon as prisoners after our people were defeated in war. Of course, from then on the victors deemed us to be slaves. Nobody talked about it. The elders knew but forbade everyone from mentioning it. It was a taboo to reveal the secret because they might have felt it reflected poorly on the enslaved and the enslavers.

I told Vera what had happened. On a free day she went home to protest. She thanked Daddy and Madam for their ejection of the insulting bush people, but wanted them to give their consent explicitly.

"He will be my husband, not my houseboy," Vera told her parents.

She wanted to eliminate an embarrassment she felt her parents might have because I was once their servant.

"No, that's unfair of you. After all, he was your teacher from elementary school through your secondary school," Daddy told her.

"I am happy you know that. He has been the person closest to me and he has been my greatest helper. Don't separate us," she pleaded.

Daddy and Madam knew that our union was inevitable but still put up a weak fight of wills. Vera stopped eating. Mummy was the first to acquiesce to our proposal. It was she who whittled Daddy's belated resistance. She recounted to him how young ladies had killed themselves for being refused to marry men of their choice by their parents.

"Let them do what they want," Daddy told her.

That was the reluctant but open consent we needed. A month later we married in court in Warri, leaving for the future the traditional rites and church services. We knew the traditional side would be difficult but Daddy assured us that we did not need to go to Agbon but the bride-price paying ceremony should take place in his house. After all, he was the oldest man in his family since his father died. And it was his blessing anyway that we needed, not of people in the village.

We rejoiced that we had won a difficult battle and would live happily together for the rest of our lives. But who can tell the future, who knows tomorrow? In Warri, the storm came without clouds, or clouds swooped in like a hawk, and before you got time to seek shelter, it had already broken out and done its destruction. We were not armed for what happened to separate us forever.

We shelved the traditional and church rites and continued with our married life. Vera had a normal pregnancy term, but the delivery eternally separated us, leaving me to mourn.

i used to drive a mercedes

"I used to drive a Mercedes," a dishevelled man told passers-by.

He marched, almost in military precision to an imaginary martial band. However, his legs moved a little too swiftly for a ceremonial occasion. Of course, there was the absence of dignity in his restless movement. He wore no uniform but had on partly torn clothes. He would pass for a roadside motor mechanic if he did not appear too excited and uncontrollable.

"I used to drive a Mercedes. Give way and let me pass," he bellowed hoarsely.

Alfred would use his right hand to toot an invisible horn and shout "Pio-pio-pioooo!"

Passers-by looked at him and those who knew his story shook their heads. Children teased him with questions.

"Where's your Mercedes?"

"They stole it. All of you are robbers," he would shout back at the taunting kids.

At other times he told questioners who asked about where his Mercedes was,

"My wife drove it to Kano."

The children would imitate his Mercedes horn blast, and he would pursue them for a minute and stop abruptly as if he had come to a barricade.

True, Alfred used to drive a Mercedes Benz. That was a long time ago, after he recovered from initial emotional shock and professional down-turns. However, subsequent misfortunes sent him into temporary insanity, which those who knew him would say was normal considering what he had gone through. He had gone through fire, had been scalded, blistered all over, got burnt, and disfigured emotionally without dying. Many in his position might have died and would not have had the resilience to survive and now be marching in the street, providing this entertaining spectacle to adults and children.

This time his madness appeared permanent. Neither the Army he had served for twelve years nor his family paid attention to his plight anymore. He disappeared at night and reappeared in the morning. During the day, he drove his imaginary Mercedes through Ring Road, turned to Mission Road, and back.

"Why can't they take him to Uselu? Are they waiting for him to tear off his clothes and be naked before they do something for him?" some sympathizer questioned.

Uselu Clinic in the Old Lagos Road was famous for its Mental Hospital. That was the only Government-owned facility for treating mental cases around. Traditional healing homes were abundant in rural areas and the treatment in them was harsh. The mad were physically beaten so that they could calm down into wraith-like living dead.

"Maybe he's beyond cure!" a passer-by said.

"They should remove him from the street at least and take him home. He must come from somewhere," another said out of pity.

Alfred Tobrise rose from the ranks to be a Major fairly fast, bearing in mind that he graduated from the University of Ibadan and was commissioned a lieutenant in the Education Corp, a division that was notorious for low promotion of officers. He majored in English and liked romance novels and love poems. He dabbled into writing love poems and composed one for each girlfriend he had at the time. Army work had not given him the tranquility he needed to write other poems before his problems overwhelmed him. He married three years after his graduation because he was tired of moving from one woman to another.

Major Alfred Tobrise adored his beautiful wife, Sarah. He felt lucky that he had married so beautiful a woman. He liked being seen with her and he felt satisfied that his wife was the most beautiful not only in the barracks but also in his battalion and division. It was not difficult to observe Major Tobrise's elevation of his wife to the status of a goddess, not of fortune but one whose beauty he had to keep on maintaining. One has to work on beauty to sustain it, he felt. She bought cosmetics and fashionable dresses and looked great in them.

As Major Tobrise's relations saw it, their son was in his wife's pocket and they predicted that a marriage in which a man worshipped his wife would end up hurting the man irreparably. They believed in their hearts and said it openly that Sarah had prepared some charms to make their son senseless. Udu women, they said, took care to keep their men leashed to their waists. A fowl would always go round a bottle of corn. Once you marry an Udu woman, you will be lost to your relations and friends, they said. Because of the nature of the bond between Alfred and Sarah, the man's people and friends stopped visiting him at home.

In the Army in which bonding was cultivated, just in case a coup by colleagues could land one in a big position, Major Alfred Tobrise was seen by his course mates as squandering away his energy and prospects for the future by cultivating only the friendship of his wife, to whose comfort he devoted all his attention. He bought her nice and expensive clothes and she dazzled in them.

Sarah had no doubt that her husband cared for her. A Grade II Teacher, she pressed Major Tobrise to send her to the University. Those who got Teachers' Grade II Certificate with her had gone to and graduated from various universities. Sarah felt all the fine clothes she had could not make up for a degree. Introduce yourself as an alumna of So-and-so University and you were respected. It was as if other graduate women knew that she was not a graduate, hence they always talked about their degrees on social occasions. A degree was what others had that she lacked. Once she had got it, she would be thrice a lady; beautiful, rich, and educated.

She detailed how she could start a business when she graduated.

"I'm not going to study, get a degree, and work for anybody," Sarah told Alfred.

"That will be fantastic. Form a company and run it," he suggested.

Alfred went along with Sarah's requests and she knew this would be the case even before she made her requests.

"Dear, you can read my mind," she told Alfred.

"I know what is good for you and me," he quipped.

"A contracting firm, a building firm, so many things, beside poultry, to do to earn more money," she said.

Already Major Tobrise had a big poultry farm in Oghara, Midway Poultry, which he had started with money meant for an unexecuted project but which he had claimed with the state governor's approval. Once or twice a week he visited the poultry to check on sales and the health of the birds. He always brought home two dozen eggs and two already prepared chickens. Sarah loved eggs and chicken. She could not imagine herself eating tough beef or anything else than chicken.

"Chicken is my stuff," she boasted to fellow members of NAOWA, the officers' wives' association.

As they say in Army circles, Major Alfred Tobrise pressed all the necessary buttons and Sarah entered the University to study Business Management.

In the university, Sarah Tobrise saw her horizon open into new vistas. Despite her husband's protests, she insisted on staying in the women's hostel on weekdays and coming home only on weekends. She skipped some weekends when, according to her, she had many assignments to complete.

Sarah learnt fast in the classroom and in the women's hall. She blamed herself for being too timid for so long.

"I'm glad my eyes are now open," she told herself.

She thought she had been fashionable, but now she saw that the Army Barracks' fashion was no fashion at all. In the university, you met and saw sophisticated women whose dresses and perfumes invited men to adore them. She soon knew boutiques and stores where high-society things were bought. She asked Alfred for money to purchase the latest fashion and indulge her growing appetite for trendy wear.

It was difficult to know that she was married because she did not behave differently from the single girls. She wore no ring, since, according to her, that was a sign of bondage. She spent time outside the class in the company of fashionable ladies and they went to parties. When she heard stories from other ladies of Marks and Spencer, a superstore in London, she made up her mind to go on a summer vacation. She did not want to lack any experience that others used in promoting themselves at her expense. If you were a student and a lady and you had not gone on summer vacation to London, you were not yet a full lady. She wanted no incompleteness in her life. She wanted to be at the same height with or higher than others.

The next weekend she was home. Major Tobrise felt loved when she said she had assignments but wanted to be with him. As a married woman, she said, she knew she had to make some sacrifices for her marriage. At night as she watched a video musical, *La vie est belle*, with Alfred, she broached her plans.

"Al, I want a ticket for a summer vacation in London," she told him with the assurance of a woman who knew she could not be denied her desire.

Alfred was at first taken aback because she had never called him Al before. However, he felt Al must be Alfred for short and it was said so endearingly.

"When?" Alfred asked.

"Al, now. This coming summer," she said.

She got her ticket and Major Tobrise took her to Lagos for her British Airways midnight flight to London Gatwick.

The details of her vacation are sketchy in parts. The true story of how she met Alhaji Isa Mohammed, a young millionaire from Kano, at Marks and Spencer will perhaps not be fully told. One of the single ladies she flew out with said Sarah behaved in a very avaricious manner. She spent the little money she brought the first day she was at Marks and Spencer. That was before her eyes opened to London to see more of Marks and Spencer and huge sales in Oxford Street and Liverpool Street Market.

Sarah Tobrise vied with single girls for Alhaji Isa Mohammed's heart and won convincingly. She did not care about the insults they poured on her as a prostitute. She said all of them who came on the summer vacation were prostitutes and she was not worse than any other in their company. She did not want to fail in whatever she had set her mind on. She wanted to have a big slice of London and take it home for exhibition. The whole of Nigeria would come to admire her taste for good things.

Isa who had not been so treated by a woman of Sarah's beauty, education, and experience lavished his unlimited foreign exchange on his love. The Warri Youth Corper he slept with five years earlier was a plaything compared to Sarah. He had money and wanted his money to give him pleasure. There was no greater pleasure for him in all his life than Sarah's body.

Sarah left her group and moved into Isa's hotel room at the Tudor's. The hotel mesmerized her and she became Isa's "wonder girl."

"My wonder girl," Isa would call her, asking, "Where will you want us to go tomorrow?"

"To St. Anne's Park," she would say.

At another time it was Madame Toussaud's Wax Museum, Trafalgar Square, and the London Zoo, names of places of attraction she had gleaned from a tourist pamphlet. Alhaji Isa Mohammed phoned for a taxi to take them wherever they wanted. At the Wax Museum, Isa complimented her with "You are my Cleopatra, Sarah."

"Thank you, my dear," she answered.

Sarah felt she was in a honeymoon with Isa who spoilt her with affection and money. Sarah gave back affection with both hands. She was like a teenager again, full of excitement and energy for love. She felt she had in a short while gained back the loss of excitement in so many years of traditional love she has had in marriage. She did not know love could be so intoxicating, more so than the red wine they drank in their room.

The four weeks passed as if they were one week. Isa followed Sarah in the Victoria Station Express to Gatwick and went as far as the Immigration Control before turning back. Both promised to meet in a specified guest house in Ibrahim Taiwo Road, Kano, in a week.

Sarah did not care that though in the same flight with her colleagues, they never exchanged any words in the plane. If I had not got Isa, one of them would have stolen the golden man for herself, she told herself. She dismissed their behaviour as petty jealousy. She went to war with them and she has been victorious. Let the defeated rivals weep over their losses, let them behave like children who lost a simple game of survival. She no longer had time for them. They would all be graduates and she would have the money and the beauty always to outshine them in any contest.

Major Alfred Tobrise was open-mouthed at what his wife brought back from London. Different types of laces, brocade, dresses, wrappers, perfumes, creams, and others. She said her uncles and cousins were so generous to her. Major Tobrise so much loved his wife that he did not question her excuses for the many things she bought.

Sarah's taste was now insatiable. She wanted to live with Major Tobrise as if she was still with Alhaji Isa Mohammed in a London hotel. She suddenly travelled out, according to her, to visit her girlfriends in Kano. She kept the tryst with Isa and returned after five days of tumultuous love-making.

By the time she was leaving Kano for Benin, she knew her marriage with Major Tobrise was over. Sarah made so many impossible demands that the major could not meet.

"Why can't we once in a while go to a hotel to pass the weekend, have real fun rather than be bored at home?" she asked.

"Are you bored the few days you spend with me?" the major asked back.

"How will you know that I am bored, you Urhobo man? What do you know about living an exciting life? I bet you are not better than those people in the village," she told him.

Alfred was not bothered that his wife had become very stylish in many ways. As an undergraduate and one who had been to London, her tastes were bound to change, he convinced himself. But Sarah taunted him with what he could not yet afford.

"Major for nothing. See your mates with Mercedes for their wives while I am still on *footroen* and you driving a

Beetle," she complained.

"With time I will buy a Mercedes. I am just a major but I am already trying my best with the poultry farm," he explained.

"I won't enter that Beetle again," she swore.

Sarah left Major Tobrise like a girlfriend leaving a boyfriend. In her last year in the university, she never went to Major Tobrise's on weekends. Rather she flew to Kano. What of the bride price that Major Tobrise had paid to marry her? She made statements that she knew would reach the major to the effect that she knew he needed money more than herself and that she could send him a cheque for the amount he had paid. The first half of her statement annoyed Major Tobrise and made him forget about the refund of the bride price. Moreover, he still felt that with time Sarah could change her mind or see reason to come back to him. After all, he thought, they had had a good time together until very recently.

Major Tobrise remained in shock for months and did not accept that Sarah had left him for good. Alone at home, he called her name as if that would make her come back. He had heard of Bini and Urhobo medicine-men who made charms or cast spells to bring men back to women, and such medicine-men could bring back women to their men, he believed. He soon dismissed the idea as he felt that Sarah had become too sophisticated to be affected by such charms. She had flown to London and she was now beyond reach of native medicines. He discovered when he looked for her pictures that there was none left in the house. No doubt she wanted to be totally out of his house and life. But she could not take away her memory from him and that haunted him daily.

Major Tobrise was no longer the smart officer that his superiors used to praise. His colleagues knew what was happening to him and discussed him when he was not around.

Most of them had foreseen the collapse of his marriage and very few pitied him when it inevitably happened. He indulged his wife in luxuries and he lost her to the lifestyle he promoted but could not sustain, they said.

Major Tobrise took a decision. He was going to buy a Mercedes. Let Sarah see him driving a Mercedes and come back to him. He felt buying a Mercedes was the charm that would reverse his failed marriage into fresh love. To buy a Mercedes, he needed a lot of money and the only money he had was in kind, Midway Poultry Farm, which had to be converted into ready cash. He would not mind if somebody would give him a Mercedes in place of his poultry, but he realized that the age of trade by barter was long gone. He decided to sell everything in Midway Poultry Farm from eggs, chickens, to feed and cages

Fortunately, he got somebody to buy his poultry farm. Poultry was a lucrative business as many of the rich would continue to have breakfast of eggs and dinner of chicken. How could somebody with a poultry farm give it away for a mere five hundred and fifty thousand, only half a million naira? Only desperate need could drive the proprietor of such a farm to sell it at a time when the poultry business was booming and expensive to start. But elders know that the farmer who sells his prize yam must be needy; if not, he would have kept it for himself. Alfred's immediate need was available cash for a Mercedes.

The major took two soldiers in an Army jeep to collect his payment and say goodbye to Midway Poultry Farm. He got his payment, stacks of naira, five hundred and fifty thousand naira, enough for him to buy a good used Mercedes. He was glad that now he could realize his dream of driving a Mercedes Benz at last but sad that he had lost part of himself, the farm which had become like a second home to him. This was the money that transformed so much in life. People loved for money, people betrayed for money. Money was such a powerful god, he told himself.

On his way back to the barracks at Ekenwan quarter of Benin, he stopped at the university to ask of Ekaite Okon whom he had met several days earlier. If Sarah had felt because she was an undergraduate and now too important to be his wife, he too could date undergraduate girls. After all, before his marriage he had as girlfriends many beautiful girls. He was unlike most of the officers who did not have university education before joining the army because he had seen, as he saw it, all there was in the university at Ibadan.

That contemplated twenty-minute stop at the Female Hall brought Major Tobrise face to face with death and scars that would trail him in the street. He revived from seeming death, but never as a sane man again.

At the Female Hall's Porters' Lodge, Major Alfred Tobrise asked to see Miss Ekaite Okon. The Female Hall officials took their time. Nigerian Army officers were not used to waiting to be attended to. More so, by women. The porters were opening drawers and pulling out files leisurely. They had just started their late afternoon shift. Major Tobrise grew impatient.

"How long do I have to wait?" he asked.

"Which of the Ekaite Okons do you want?" they asked him.

"Just call me Ekaite Okon," he retorted.

"Okay, write your name down and sign so that we'll send for any or both of them," they told him in the manner of doing their duty.

"I don't have to write my name anywhere. You bloody civilians, get me Ekaite!" he ordered.

"We are not here to call girls for men," one of them suppressing her anger told him.

"Then what are you paid for?" he asked.

"You don't pay me," another porter told him.

"If the Government pays you, I am part of the Government and so I pay you," he told her.

"If you are Government, you are not my Vice-Chancellor, Registrar, or Bursar," she replied.

"For how long do you have to gossip and talk nonsense rather than do your work?" he queried.

The more rude questions he asked, the more stubborn the portresses became. The three women ignored him to attend to new arrivers. Major Tobrise stopped them from attending to others. At this time the Student Union President, Paul Ighodaro, appeared and asked what the problem was.

Before any of the portresses could open their mouths to explain, Major Tobrise exploded.

"Get out of here," he ordered.

The Student Union President maintained his cool and asked whether the major was asking to see his wife.

"No, he wants one of the Ekaites," they told him.

"One of the Okons?" he asked.

"Mr. Whoever-You-Are, it's enough. Leave these women to call me Miss Ekaite Okon," he said with visible irritation.

"Let them do their work the way they were told to do it," the student president tried to explain.

"Shut your mouth there. I attended U.I., the premier university, not this high school slum of a university," Major Tobrise told the student president.

Paul Ighodaro flared up like an explosion. He felt not only himself but also his university were being slighted and he had to defend the honour of his great university. In a scuffle which ensued, Major Tobrise, unarmed, was overpowered and floored by several men and women. The students were enraged at being insulted in their own institution and meted their bitter vengeance on Major Tobrise.

An angry student mob could do the most savage of things. They did not spare the major any of the violence that angry students were wont to unleashing on their victims. They were patriots defending the honour of their republic, the University of Benin. Was it not here that student cultists killed three policemen a year earlier? Was it not here that a female student who failed to be intimidated into sex by a cult member was acidized and deformed in her most private part? These students could look good but were barbarians when provoked. Major Tobrise had stirred the hornets' nest and he must suffer the sting of their wrath.

The students sprayed insecticide on the major and he writhed in pain, in a delirium. Meanwhile one of the hall officials pointed out that he came in an army jeep. Students surged there and with the two soldiers fleeing for their lives, set the jeep on fire. The jeep and what was inside, the bundles of naira, were consumed by flames fuelled by kerosene.

In the campus melee, campus police arrived early enough to save Major Tobrise from the students' ultimate act of anger. His shirt and trousers were torn, but their primary concern was for his life rather than his dress. Who cares about the whereabouts of the hat when the head itself is falling? The campus police took pity on him, asked him questions about his home and learning he was in the Army, put him in a taxi to his barracks.

For three days Major Tobrise locked himself in. He was not aware of being asleep or being awake those days. He was also not aware of hunger or thirst. His head was light and then heavy. He had visions of Sarah kissing him, stripping before him but denying him sex, which led them to struggle in the process of which he hit his head against the wall. He was not aware of time, neither of day nor of night. He remained in what in his vision was his bunker, where nobody could do him any harm.

When he finally opened his door, he held a rifle and headed for the Deputy Adjutant's home. He broke into a trot, then walked briskly. It was evening and he expected the Deputy Adjutant whom he described as a coward to be in. Only cowards hide behind their wives and children when they ought to be fighting a battle of honour, he reflected. He would prove his courage today and after his heroic act he would be carried shoulder-high by other officers for doing them proud. He imagined himself in the parade ground taking the salute from his superiors in the force.

Soon he was before the Deputy Adjutant's house. Still wielding his gun like a firebrand, he stood in the manner of one about to aim a shot.

"When I was being attacked, you didn't come to my rescue. What type of Adjutant are you?" he shouted.

"Coward, come out," he shouted in an even louder voice.

He knocked as if he wanted to break the door. The Deputy Adjutant had seen him from a window and ducked flat. In the barracks anything could happen and officers had to expect death at close range without warning. The Deputy Adjutant had seen and heard of soldiers and officers who went beserk and fired at people indiscriminately. He was always on guard. He had seen the disraught major from afar coming and he sensed the worst from him. He was lucky that he could read minds and faces fast. Major Tobrise fired the gun at the door and turned back, thinking there was nobody in.

Major Tobrise had serious questions to answer in the Army. How did a jeep meant for official assignments get to be parked by the female student hall of residence in the university? How did this jeep supposed to be guarded by two soldiers get burnt? Where did he get the kind of rifle he fired?

Did he fire at his superior officer? And with what intent did he fire?

An investigative tribunal was set up comprising five officers, three colonels and two lieutenant colonels. Major Tobrise appeared as he must, but he was defiant.

"I fired at the Deputy Adjutant's door. He did not come to my rescue when I was being attacked," he told the tribunal.

"What did you intend to do?" they asked.

"I don't know. I only know I wanted to shoot him for failing to rush to my rescue. How can he allow those bloody civilians to beat an officer and get away with it?" he asked.

"Did he or the Army send you to the female hall of residence?" the tribunal asked him.

"Why do you ask me such questions? Whether I went to eat goat-head, take pepper-soup, or visit Ekaite Okon, it is none of your business," he shouted at the officers questioning him.

"Major Tobrise, maybe you don't understand what we are asking. If you went to take pepper-soup or to visit Ekaite Okon, it was your private business and why did you use an Army jeep and why did you expect to be rescued by the Army if it is none of the Army's business?" the Chair of the investigative panel asked him.

"You are on his side. You are not listening to me. I thought he would come out and I would have executed him on behalf of the Army for not coming to my rescue," he told them.

The tribunal's work was made easy by his persistent acceptance of firing with vengeful arrogance. Verdict: strong grounds for court martial.

The court martial was swift. For taking the Army jeep for an unauthorized trip, getting it burnt, and attempting to assassinate the Deputy Adjutant, Major Tobrise was discharged with ignominy from the Nigerian Army. Many felt that his good standing in the army before his problem mitigated against a harsher sentence. If he aimed at the Deputy Adjutant, he had wanted to kill and a stiffer punishment might have condemned him to death by firing squad. He accepted the verdict, which he could not appeal against. It was only the General Officer Commanding the Division who could change the verdict, but Major Tobrise felt he would not beg anybody in the Army which has ruined his life for anything. If he had joined another profession after graduating from Ibadan so many years ago, he might have gone far in the civil service or in the private sector. He felt a surge of bitterness against those he called half-illiterates in the Nigerian Army who formed the senior officer cadres and who did not want the university educated officers to rise beyond the rank of lieutenant colonel. Illiterates leading the educated. Major Tobrise said he would not condescend to beg an illiterate officer to reduce his sentence. He was ready to weather it, he told himself. Since he was not jailed and only discharged from the army, there was life still ahead for him, he reflected.

Major Tobrise was a pitiful man after being discharged. Not that he had been good-looking since his wife abandoned him. He had no savings and he looked very wretched. He was hurriedly moved out of his Army quarters and he had to look for a two-room apartment in a low-cost area of Benin.

Within six months of his discharge, Major Tobrise (rtd.) was barely hanging to life. Because he was discharged, he had no money paid him either as gratuities, emoluments, or pension. People shook their heads at how he fell from high society to low life. Fellow officers who saw his pitiable condition reported to their superiors. Through goodwill, it was announced that his case would be reviewed.

The review like everything about Major Alfred Tobrise was swift. His discharge with ignominy was converted to retirement and backdated. He collected a huge lump sum, two hundred and fifty thousand naira. This time he acted promptly. He collected his money and went straight to buy one of those *tokunbo* cars, also called *Belgium*, a used Mercedes. In fact, only five hundred naira was left of his emoluments after buying and licensing the car. That was barely enough for him to fill the tank to take the car home.

Still Major Tobrise (rtd.) was visibly happy. Not well dressed but in his rattling Mercedes, he beamed smiles and waved to those he didn't even know. In his mind, he saw Sarah coming back and after giving her a ride in the Mercedes, staying put with him. After all, she wanted me to buy a Mercedes and I have got it, he reasoned. He had heard that Sarah was driving a Mercedes bought for her by one man. If she came back, he would give this Mercedes to her and work to buy another. But he did not know where Sarah was and could not reach her to tell her that he had bought the desired Mercedes.

Three weeks after Major Tobrise (rtd.) bought his Mercedes, it broke down in the middle of nowhere on the Lagos-Benin Road. It was almost dark on a road that was prone to armed robbers. He carried no gun to defend himself. He had attempted to get a gun license but was denied because of his past army record of carrying a gun without permit, and attempting to assassinate a senior officer. The retired major was scared, not just for his life but for his car. Now that he had bought the car of his dreams, he wanted to live to enjoy driving it. No driver stopped to give him a ride. When he waved, the drivers accelerated the more. After what he calculated was up to a hundred futile attempts to stop a passing driver for help, he tried to give thought to his condition.

At first he wanted to sleep in the car till the next morning when other drivers would be less suspicious of somebody by the roadside asking for help. He dismissed the idea, believing he might get a mechanic and still drive the car away that night. He decided to trek to Ore whose distance he could not tell. At Ore he would get a mechanic and come back to repair the car or have it towed to a secure place. That trek was the learning experience of what would be his daily treks through streets of Benin. He had forgotten it was Sunday and there was no mechanic around at eight-thirty, unlike on weekdays when they worked till eleven.

By the next morning when he was back with a mechanic to fix the car, he could not believe what he saw. It was not his Mercedes but a scarecrow metallic body. All the car tyres were gone. The front and rear windscreens were gone. Gone too were the dashboard, the steering, the axle, and the exhaust pipes. The Mercedes Benz was thoroughly cannibalized.

Major Alfred Tobrise (rtd.) must have trekked from what used to be his car to Benin, a distance of seventy miles, without talking to anybody. He did not go to his home again.

"I used to drive a Mercedes," he told people in a town which was now strange to him. Ever since, he had been wandering in Benin, blowing his imaginary horn and shouting at passersby, saying

"I used to drive a Mercedes."

God's medicine-men

They lived in Igbi Street and we lived in Ginuwa Road. Igbi Street runs into Ginuwa Road where my father's house still stands. My friend's home was less than five minutes walk from ours. From childhood, we played in the same churchyard, the Anglican mission. We children did not know any difference between the Catholic and Anglican churches as our parents did. Endurance's father was a pastor, an Anglican reverend. My father was a churchman of the Catholic faith and he went daily to Mass in the cathedral a half-mile away. After school, the open Anglican school ground was ours for play till we were tired. We girls played together, so we established a common bond.

Even though we went to different elementary schools, we ended up in the same Government Teachers' College at Bomadi for our Grade II Teacher's Certificate. Government was neither Anglican nor Catholic, so those of us who went to different denominational elementary schools converged in a government-run teachers' college. We girls in the college were not many and so knew ourselves very well. For me and Endurance who came from the same town and had known each other and played together for years, it appeared we were from the same family.

That's how we became even closer and I got to know not only Endurance's father but also Odele, two of God's medicine-men. That's how I also came to see Endurance's disappointing marriage as partly caused by me even though in the end people should make their own choices. I thought I was helping my friend but I could have been playing the matchmaker without knowing.

Whenever Endurance was going to bed, she always double-checked to ensure that the doors were properly secured. Though it was unusual to padlock the door from inside, her parents allowed her to do so. They believed their daughter was paranoid and hoped her fears would subside with more years. It was not that she was afraid that burglars would break in, but she could not identify the source of what was happening to her. She was determined to stop a burglary of another kind.

It was vacation time when her two other sisters and her brother were around. She shared one room with her sisters and so she did not sleep alone. She slept in one bed, but there were two other beds in the room. Even when she changed beds with her junior sisters, there was no reprieve from the strange intruder. And yet she was always on her guard.

Her mind travelled in all directions. Where could this stranger come from to be able to enter into her at will? She knew that for all the quarrels they had in daytime and which were tightly hidden from outsiders, her father and mother slept together. After all, what would the congregation think of a pastor who quarrelled with his wife? What kind of example the church's First Couple would be giving if their exchange of insults was heard outside their home? But they fired abuses at each other in low tones and their voices were never raised to reach the street.

Endurance marvelled at her parents' self-control in bottling up their fracas. While she hated their squabbles, she admired the limits they placed upon themselves. Quarrel, but let no outsider hear of it. Quarrel, but put on a cheerful face for the world to see. Sleep in the same room and the same bed but ignore the other as much as possible for the children not to know that they did not really sleep together. They had to give a good example not only as a good and happy couple but also as good and happy parents.

There were two men in the house at night: her father and

her sibling brother. She could not imagine the impossible, that her father or brother could be the one. There were certain things she did not want to think about and suspecting her own father or brother was ruled out. Endurance was at a loss on what to do.

She was twenty-one and had made love several times before. She knew as a pastor's daughter she had to hide to have her fill in this respect. Her mother and father might think she was still a virgin, but she could not afford to let them know any better. Being a pastor's daughter, she had little chance of going out, and no young man had the courage to come to see her in her father's house.

Their five-bedroom mansion stood at one corner of the mission grounds which also held an elementary school and a big church. Painted brown like the school and church buildings, their house was impressive in size. Endurance and her sisters and brother felt fortunate about their home because they could tell from their friends' homes that theirs was indeed a very big house. They have seen their friends live with their parents in one or two-room apartments.

She made sure that she wore tight underwear to bed, but that did not stop the intruder from entering into her at will. She wore trousers to bed, and yet she woke with a feeling of sticky wetness between her legs.

As a beautiful young woman of twenty-one, she was attracted to some men, but none of them had made any serious effort to win her love. Her fear and frustration had been this secret stealing into her and waking without remembering anything but only to see the wet and sticky mess between her legs. She has had faint recollections of her ecstasy, but there was no face to place on the man who came into her in her dream. She would not mind sleeping with somebody who loved her and whose face and name she recognized. But she hated this robber who secretly took away from her, her most private possession.

She was scared for her life. Somebody or spirit was in control of her life and she could become what she had not planned for herself. If some man or spirit made love with her successfully, would she not be pregnant? Will her parents, especially her father, believe her innocence, or will they blow out for being scandalized by their supposedly wayward daughter? After all, he always preached against young girls and boys for not following the ways of Christ and knowing what they should not know before they got married. Will they understand the strange phenomenon? But why not, if they knew of the Virgin Mary? Endurance acknowledged that though she was a pastor's daughter, she did not have the spirituality of the Holy Mother. Strange things could always happen. But she was not a virgin--she lost that in, of all places, the village where she and her sisters had gone to spend a vacation. There she had been as free as air and her grandfather and grandmother had treated them so specially that they would like to live with them all the time. But she was already a grown-up girl who must go to school.

Recently, when her mother and father travelled out of town, she sat in the sitting room and since she was the eldest child and in control, nobody told her to go to bed. She fell asleep on the couch and woke after another orgasm. Her thighs as usual were sticky with thick wetness.

She thought seriously of buying contraceptives from one of the many pharmacists in the town. She had to protect herself, and she knew all she had to do was to ask for a packet of contraceptive pills with one hand, while handing over the money to the pharmacist with the other hand. After all, nobody would recognize her since the pharmacists had the habit of not looking their customers in the face. They avoided visual contacts because all they cared for was their money. They did not want to have to do anyone any favour on the basis of facial recognition. So they avoided it.

But Endurance was not a stranger to strange experiences.

She had come home from school to solve a problem, only to face a more intractable one. At school she had been helpless before a succubus. That was what they called the invisible person who came to press her while she slept at night. Again, this person was not barred by sealed school doors. Even though she shared a room with four other girls, she was the only one who experienced the incubus or succubus, whatever that oppressive spirit was called.

At first she was quiet over the experience which came at long intervals, but later when the frequency increased she could no longer bear the burden without crying out. She told me as her bosom friend about it but I did not have much to say then. What does the daughter of a Catholic Head Christian know about spirits pressing people down at night in their sleep? That was before I spent one of the long holidays with my aunt in Benin. Children of Christian parents, we had been discouraged from believing in the supernatural. We grew up to believe that there were Satanic forces, evil spirits, that could be overwhelmed by constant prayers to God.

"In the name of Christ, I stop you. With the blood of Jesus, I overrule you," Endurance had chanted many times.

However, like the new evil spirit, the incubus persisted and refused to be annihilated by either the name or blood of Christ or Jesus. She lit candles in the room but the incubus bypassed the candles and still stole in to press her. She placed a Bible beneath her pillow, but the incubus was not scared by the Holy Book; it still pressed her while asleep on the bed.

"Why me, God?" Endurance had asked many times.

"Continue to pray for help," I told her.

I knew that my friend must be going through a very difficult situation, but I did not know of any solution. Endurance was getting more distracted than usual and the former bubbling Black Princess, Warri Queen, as she was popularly called, was losing much of her lustre. It has been because of Endurance's case that I know that worries could hurt more than physical sickness. If she had suffered from malaria or something else, the doctor who visited our college twice a week would have cured her. But this was not a case she could bring to the young doctor who chased many female students who visited him to cook and do other things for him.

It was these strange experiences that drove the pastor's daughter, my good friend, to seek help from her friends.

This was her final year in the two-year programme. She decided to go home and tell her parents what was happening to her. She had to tell the matron and the principal why she needed to go home early. The teachers' college encouraged discipline and the principal did not want students to leave for home individually. During vacations, they went home in groups and that was safer than being alone. Of course, while I and mutual friends knew about her condition, she also needed to explain to her other friends what was driving her home so early.

We had always cherished our camaraderie--gosssiping about other female students and their teachers and male students, recollecting common adventures, and other things that bound us together as young girls.

But Endurance realized that she did not really need to explain her problems to the whole world. She thought that when she was back at home the aura of prayers would drive away the evil spirit that tormented her. So she had to manufacture a reason to the Principal and she got her permission to leave.

The boat journey home on the Warri river always frightened her. She did not know how to swim, but she spent ten hours on the wide river that was notorious for crocodiles, sharks, and big fishes that wrecked small boats. A few students had been victims of the vast and deep river, which yearly had its casualties. The current was violent in the salt side of the river. The boat was not as packed full as when she travelled with her fellow students. Then the boatmen filled the boats like the slave ships they read about in their history books to make the maximum profit and did not care if the boat sank from overweight. By the time they had come to the fresh water side of the river, she knew she was close to home. The river was narrower, less angry, and had more villages on the banks. Endurance's breath became more relaxed and she started planning how she would tell her mother and father about her problem.

At home she could not immediately tell them about it. She was in a dilemma. On one level, her father railed against evil spirits, witches, and demons in his sermons. In other words, these wicked forces existed to be fought and defeated. On the other hand, she as a Christian was supposed to believe that none of the wicked forces could have power over her as long as she believed in the power of Christ. She believed in God and Jesus who came to the world to save humankind, but that belief had not driven away the incubus that tormented her nightly. She was not sure of how her father in particular would respond to her talking about being pressed at night and she was afraid of being accused of believing in the power of demons rather than of Christ whose blood could wash away all evils. For these uncertainties she told her parents that she was sick, always dizzy and feeling like fainting.

My friendship with Endurance made me to know the Anglican pastor very well. I saw him frequently and as children of the same street, we heard stories about him. People say he had gone to Jerusalem a long time ago. I believe this because Endurance confirmed it and even showed me one of the silver or imitative silver cups he brought from the Holy Land. Some photographs of Christ on the walls of their sitting room were quite unique and could have come only from the Holy Land.

Pastor Efe in many ways had lived up to the expectations of his wealthy name. How could anyone have predicted that the first son of a traditional healer that the white missionaries had condemned to hell before his death would become the pastor of a major diocese. Pastor Jeremiah Efe had confounded village pundits. Even his own father who had hoped that the son would take over the healing trade from him just as he had taken it over from his own father, no longer felt betrayed. He did not visit his son on Sundays but he saw the big church at the other end of the field in the big compound that his son virtually owned in the name of God. Of course, his pastor son had not visited him on *edewor*, the traditional day of worship, when his home was full of patients needing assistance.

Pastor Jeremiah Efe had gone to school and distinguished himself in the old Standard Six, and a series of missionary schools for would-be pastors had made him very learned. From his preachings, one could tell that he knew the Bible very well. He quoted effortlessly from the Old and the New Testaments. He not only knew the verses but also the very page numbers of his quotes from the King James Version that his church used. He told his congregation that despite being a busy pastor, he read the entire Bible every year, which meant he had read the Bible twenty times or more since he answered the pastoral call.

His congregation loved him, mainly because he was seen as a happily married man of a good family. And he preached very well. He railed against witches, evil-doers, and wicked spirits in the strongest of terms. He could move people to tears and laughter with his words. He got possessed once the sermon began and the Holy Spirit spoke through his tongue. He spoke simple Urhobo-laced English, which worked well with most of his congregation, illiterate, semi-literate, and highly literate alike. Men and women, young and old, all were solidly attached to his church, and this meant that Sunday worship at St. Matthew's was a fulfilling experience to pastor and congregation.

The white Bishop in Benin must have heard many good things said about Pastor Jeremiah Efe, apart from his own favourable impression of the fine young man, so that when the Archbishop of Canterbury created an opportunity for his

"Nigerian brothers" to visit the Holy Land, he was easily picked as one of the native pastors in the contingent.

Pastor Jeremiah Efe visited Jerusalem in 1971. Jerusalem. The Holy Land. The Stone City. The City of Golden Sunset. The Birthplace of Jesus. The experience remained fresh in his mind. The son of an Urhobo traditional healer in the Land of Miracles! He has not forgotten the Wailing Wall, where he put on a Jewish skullcap and scribbled prayers which he tucked into the cracks of the old wall. He wanted to rise to be Bishop. He wanted peace in his home. He wanted his church to grow big, and overflow with worshippers. At the Church of the Holy Sepulchre, he visited different chapels and saw the unity of all churches. He even went to Asqua Mosque and was overwhelmed by the grandeur of this other religion. He wondered why christians and muslims in Nigeria frequently clashed violently when, in fact, they were worshipping the same God. He saw the make-up tomb of Christ. He followed the stations of the Cross. He wished he were there in Roman times to help Christ with the Cross as did Thaddeus. Imagine if his wife, Rebecca, had like Veronica wiped tears, sweat, or blood from Jesus's body. Everything had a certain aura of sacredness.

But years later, it was the Arab market that gave him the memento of his life. He bought five silver-looking cups. In fact, the Arab trader had told him they were silver goblets. He had an obsession for these silver goblets, which he always wanted to display before his visitors.

"Drink with the cup of Christ," he told his guests once he offered them drinks.

Later, his familiar visitors got so used to being served with the cup of Christ that they asked for it, a request that became a code for drinks.

"Let me drink with one of those cups of Christ," they would request, smiling.

Of course, his visitors became many and he spent far more

than his congregation and mission paid him. Out of modesty and spiritual concerns, he was reluctant to discuss money even though he needed much more than the little he was paid. He employed innuendoes to inform members of his congregations who paid visits that his pay was not enough, but this never sank into their heads. How could anybody leaving the pastor's wealthy-looking house feel that he was close to the proverbial church rat?

"The Anglican Church is not like the Roman Catholic Church that is a state of its own and has gold reserves," he told his congregation. "We need to give to strengthen our church and ourselves," he would also add.

He was not sure whether plain talk about raising his salary would go on well with his adoring congregation. But as a pastor, Jeremiah Efe continued to entertain his church members who frequently came to visit him. It was not that he was obliged to entertain, but those cups of Christ he so much loved exhibiting made him give out drinks with both right and left hands. This was the main cause of the quiet quarrel with his wife.

"What will we use both to clothe and feed the children and also to send them to school?" she frequently asked.

"God that sent me to Jerusalem will provide for them," he would tell her.

A pastor's wife, Rebecca remained down-to-earth. She had lost her Ibo name, Ifi, to this Rebecca. Much as she told people she was Ifi, nobody was ready to call her that name. At first she felt the Urhobo did not want her to retain her real name. However, she also noticed that even the few Ibo women around also called her Rebecca or Becky. Rebecca or Ifi Efe, she was Mrs. Efe, Pastor's Wife.

I travelled to spend part of my holidays with my senior sister living with her family in Benin and during that period, through my friend, Esther, I first heard of and later met Odele. I saw Pastor Odele and knew immediately he was a strange man, but I also felt that he might be able to help my other friend Endurance to get out of her problems.

Since our parents knew we were friends, it was easy for Endurance to obtain permission from her parents to visit me and spend some time with me and my senior sister, once I sent word that I wanted her to come as soon as possible.

"Pastor Odele," as he introduced himself, projected himself as a man of piety, a man of God. He always wore a special black hat which he had never changed since the many years I knew him. The hat covered his whole head ánd left a little of the forehead. So, though he was short, you never saw his exposed head or hair. The head might be bald or the hair shaved, but I could not tell. It seemed part of his spirituality had to do with his gentlemanly and fatherly look and covering his hair. There was some power in his head covered by the hat which did not appear to wear out with time.

Pastor Odele also held a small pocket Bible almost all the time. The letters were very tiny and he must be very familiar with its content to read it without glasses. He told Esther and me that the words of the Bible were the words of God with which one could cure the worst of diseases and cast out the most wicked spirits. The combination of the special hat and the small Bible gave a certain mystique to Pastor Odele's personality. When we first came to him, we were scared but soon got used to his strangeness.

Pastor Odele was not young, somebody in his forties, I guess. Still he lived with his mother and did not appear to be married. He had a big room in his mother's house. He told us he had his own house but since we were never taken there, we felt he might be trying to avoid embarrassment for living with his mother at his age. Or he might be trying to be consciously innocuous to us, he being a man of God and we being single girls. Though he called himself a pastor, he would not take us to his church to pray as we initially thought he would do. He pointed at a distant direction where his church was, but for the months and years we would know him, none of us would ever see or enter that church.

The pastor who looked every way like a medicine-man ministered to us and other visitors who trickled into his mother's home. If the pastor's appearance frightened us at first, the inside of his mother's house gave us even a bigger fright. We looked at each other, held the other's hand and knew we could not run anywhere. There was no way, we felt, that Pastor Odele would hurt all three of us together in broad daylight in his mother's home.

Pastor Odele's mother's home was a big shrine decked with mirrors, sculptures of god-like figures, skulls, and white and red feathers. He knew we would be too scared to ask him any questions, so he tried to assure us of our safety.

"Everything on earth is made by God," he said.

We were so engrossed in the different items in the big shrine of a parlour that none of us responded to him.

"We have to fight battles with whatever arms we can muster," he told us as if he were leading the many figures of ancestors or gods to a battle that needed extraordinary weaponry.

The pastor led the three of us into his vast room which was comfortably furnished. The floor was rugged, and there were two three-seaters and a sofa--all dark blue and matching the interior painting. On the walls were pictures of Christ, *Mamiwata*, and *Ukuakpolokpolo*, the ruling Oba of Benin. There was a closet at one end of the room.

Pastor Odele asked us to sit down and feel comfortable. After Endurance told him her problems, Pastor Odele said he would take her to Sakpoba river to wash away whatever evil affected her and pray for her so that her problems would be banished forever.

We followed Pastor Odele out after he had taken whatever he went for in that closet. We went a mile or so on Sakpoba Road and turned left where the river crossed the road. We walked about five poles inside from the main road to the river which narrows before entering Benin. At this brush-covered side of the river, Pastor Odele opened one of the books of Moses, chanted in English and Edo incomprehensible lines that were meant to exorcise Endurance of evil spirits. He then asked the three of us to undress, except for our underwear; enter the water, and bathe. Meanwhile he left us alone for ten minutes or thereabouts before returning to say more prayers.

He came back when we were still in the water and did not feel embarrassed looking at our exposed breasts or body. We also felt no embarrassment since there was a purpose for our nakedness.

"Endurance, I have chased out the evil spirits pressing you or sleeping with you at night," he told a visibly relieved Endurance.

"Are you finished with me?" she asked him.

"I say in the names of Olokun and Jesus, you have been freed from bondage to evil angels," he assured her.

He then prophesyed to me that my first child would be a girl and that Esther would not marry her current boyfriend. Esther and I knew that he wanted to appear to be fair to all three of us by giving each of us something to be happy about. We were very happy that Endurance had been promised success and would be freed from both the incubus and the secret lover.

Endurance must have told her mother who told Pastor Efe about the man of God in Benin, Pastor Odele, who prayed and chased off evil spirits. As Endurance told us later, her father admitted he had feelings of a past life in which he was a medicine-man. He could smell burnt herbs, he hallucinated on seeing himself shaking rattles and invoking gods and ancestors. He was meant to take over from his father but it was too late. He could not resign from his pastoral flock to go to the village to be a full-time medicine-man.

What Endurance and her mother had thought would be a

difficult task persuading Pastor Efe to go to Benin so that
Pastor Odele could pray for them thus became so easy.

"Sometimes, the medicine-man cannot heal himself," he
told Rebecca and Endurance.

"Maybe the Benin pastor can help both of us," Rebecca
told him.

"I believe in miracles," he said.

"Amen," his wife and daughter replied in unison.

"When do we go then?" he asked.

"Whenever you are ready," they told him.

"Next Friday," he suggested.

And so Pastor Efe, his wife, and daughter went to see
Pastor Odele to pray for them. The pastor warmly received his
guests in his room in his mother's house. Pastor Efe did not
wear his pastoral collar so that he did not cut the strange figure
of a pastor in his gown in a native shrine.

As if he were a diviner, Pastor Odele told Pastor Efe his
problems before he mentioned them. And to gain his
confidence the more, he told Pastor Efe that he prayed and
made *things* for preachers so that they could overwhelm their
congregations. Pastor Efe wanted this. He took the Anglican
pastor to a corner and told him he would also solve his
problem with his wife.

They prayed together noisily and, as was common with
Pastor Odele, he invoked Olokun and Jesus Christ to inspire
Pastor Efe to preach to move people's hearts. Pastor Odele in
his hat was a medicine-man rather than a pastor. He gave
Pastor Efe two wrapped things to rub and lick before going to
bed and before going to preach. He was to do these things
without fail if he really wanted to avoid squabbles with his
wife, if he wanted his congregaton to lavishly make huge
monetary offerings, and if he wished to get promoted in his
pastoral mission.

Endurance told me that her parents became closer and had
few incidents of quarrels after their trip to Benin. The quarrels

had disappeared before Pastor Odele's visit to Warri, as he put it, for a courtesy call on Pastor Efe, a fellow man of God. He had come with his mother in his new pickup van. You could not tell that one was a medicine-woman and the other was not a pastor.

Pastor Efe, of course, wanted to be very hospitable and as usual brought out his silver goblets from Jerusalem to entertain his guests from Benin. He reported to his medicine-man, Pastor Odele, that his monthly salary was recently raised without his asking for it. He also reported about his congregation increasing, almost overflowing into the street. In addition, they were now possessed at the time of worship and gave offerings and gifts with open hands. Things could not be better than they were then with him, he reported. He thanked Pastor Odele for his prayers and everything, as he put it.

"Thank my mother," Pastor Odele told him.

"Thank you two for your prayers," Pastor Efe told his guests.

"Better things are coming into this house," Pastor Odele assured him.

"Amen," chanted Endurance's father and mother.

By the time his guests were gone, three of his silver goblets had disappeared from the cupboard where they were kept. Pastor Efe had promised his wife that he would hold back on his entertainment in order not to dissipate the new blessings of salary increase and huge offerings. So when the cups could not be found, Pastor Efe made only a feeble attempt to look for them. Then he put the remaining two in a box in his bedroom so as not to lose all of them. These will be his lifelong mementos of the pilgrimage to Jerusalem. If someday anybody doubted whether he was a JP, Jerusalem Pilgrim, he would bring them out and show the silver goblets to certify his experience.

Visitors who came with the hope of being entertained with the cups of Christ were disappointed. They were asked to join in prayers, because prayers are the greatest food of a Christian because they nourished the soul, the pastor told them. The stream of visitors that depleted their savings dried to a mere trickle and that was good for the man and woman who lived in the mission compound. That did not affect the record congregation at Sunday services.

Soon Endurance would need Pastor Odele's services and this time they would become part of each other's life for good or bad. If she was no longer being pressed by the succubus or being raped in a dream, what else could Endurance have gone to Pastor Odele to ask for? I can only string together the

pieces that my friend told me, but I knew that friends as we were, she told me the crux but not the details of what transpired between them. Sometimes we could hold back particularly embarrassing parts of a story and would expect the other to figure out the true situation. How could we at any stage have foreseen that Endurance, that Warri Queen as she was called at the Teachers' College, would make a choice that most of us were to laugh at?

As Endurance told me, she developed a certain odour which made people to avoid coming close to her. At this time we were waiting for the results of our Teacher's Grade II Certificate examination and I was again spending the free time with my senior sister in Benin. There was nothing to do till after the results when the successful ones among us would be posted to teach in elementary schools. Some of us might go straight to the university or do the National Certificate of Education programme.

I don't know the number of people who convinced Endurance that she had a very bad odour. But she said after many people had told her, she started to smell it herself. She thought it was gas and bought some medications to purge herself of the bad smell. That did not stop it. She went to a pharmacist who sold her antibiotics, terramycin and tetracyclin, but the smell did not go. She felt it came in her breath too and she found it difficult to leave home. Then she thought of Pastor Odele who had helped her before to perform more difficult tasks.

Endurance did not even come to me or Esther before going to Pastor Odele, unlike in all previous occasions when she had seen him either in our company or that of her parents. The next thing we knew was that she had informed her parents of her intention to marry somebody of her choice now that she had finished school. The person she chose to marry was Pastor Odele.

Pastor Odele had assured her that he would drive away the wicked spirits that tormented her with a repulsive body odour. He asked her to spend the night in his room in his mother's house. He would pray and also perform some sacrifices at midnight in a nearby crossroads. Before that night, Endurance told me, she had placed so much trust in Pastor Odele's power. That very night, she found herself in the experience which Pastor Odele was supposed to have cured her from. The only difference was that this time it was real. When it was over, it appeared Pastor Odele was the one who used to steal into her because it happened in the same manner. She stayed with him in Benin for three weeks without her coming to see me or Esther and while her parents thought she was with me and my sister. Imagine if something worse had happened to her in a city where ritual murderers were many! But we were lucky that bad as things appeared to me and Esther and perhaps her parents, they could have been worse.

Endurance returned to Warri but soon discovered that she was pregnant. That was how Pastor Odele came to marry Endurance, my own friend and daughter of Pastor, rather Bishop, Efe. Pastor Odele still has no church; he still wears his special hat that covers his head, lives with Endurance and their only child in his big room in his mother's house that is partly an Olokun shrine. Endurance found the three silver goblets that were missing from her father's house in Warri, but now owed allegiance to her husband than to her father and so did not report. Her father might have been surprised if told the use to which they were put at Pastor Odele's. They became part of the tools in this God's medicine-man's healing business.

But this, like many other things, did not matter now. Her father was now appointed Bishop of Benin-Delta Provinces of the Anglican Mission in Nigeria. The letter came from and was co-signed by both the Archbishop of Canterbury and the Queen and Head of the Church of England, the spiritual and political heads of the Anglican Church.

Bishop Efe moved to Benin and lived in the same town where his eldest daughter was married. They were really not married in the church or in the traditional way, but had become partners in attending to those who came to Pastor Odele or his mother for help. Endurance had become like her mother a pastor's wife, though the mother was now a bishop's wife. The Efes did not resist Endurance's choice since they believed within that Pastor Odele had done them a good turn that deserved reciprocity.

Pastor Odele's prophecies have been fulfilled. Esther broke from her boyfriend and then travelled to marry a man studying in London. We have not heard from her ever since. I have just got my first child, a girl that my husband and I have named Oghenetega. When next I travel to Benin I will visit my old friend and, maybe, both of us would visit her parents at the Bishop's Court.

the roadblock

At night Private Oyibo and Corporal Shegbe lived very luxurious lives which many above their ranks in the police would envy. With their wives they occupied separate chalets, vast and lush. No children with them, just their wives. Every night the past two months and a half, they had enjoyed themselves in Mr. Debo Fakade's best kept secret property, a five-chalet guest-house whose grounds are fenced. Many so-called big men in Warri had guest-houses scattered all over town, always far away from their own homes. After all, the guest-house was where they retreated secretly to meet their girlfriends when they were supposed to be out of town or gone to visit their male friends.

Mr. Debo Fakade was no ordinary government worker who relied on the monthly salary. As Superintendent of Prisons in charge of Warri Central Prison, he ran what his rivals and subordinates called a gold mine. Only a select few in Nigeria ran such gold mines, even though every government worker from the office messenger up wanted to gain access to the mine for some gold dust of their own.

The guest-house had its employees. There was a prisoner who Superintendent Fakade deemed not dangerous and so used to maintain the grounds, clear and clean the yard, wash clothes for the guests, and run errands if needed. He also acted as a gateman, pulling the gate open when he saw Mr. Fakade's car. Since the two guests came there, the gate-man received strict orders to open the gate only for the proprietor of the guest-house, Superintendent Fakade.

A cook served the guests. An elderly man who had served Roman Catholic priests now returned to Ireland, he had considered himself lucky to cook for guests who were never many. He got his regular salary and tips that more than doubled the salary of a government worker with his primary six education. Kevin Ovie prepared for his guests whatever dishes they wanted. Most times they asked for traditional foods, *banga* soup, *egusi* and *eba*, okra soup and pounded yam, yam and pepper soup. Occasionally they ate fried-rice, *dodo*, and fresh fish. When their wives indulged them, the guests took fried potatoes and salad. Mr. Fakade always gave Kevin enough money to stock up his supplies of foodstuffs.

You would not from their lifestyles know that these two guests were policemen and were awaiting trial. They had a serious case pending, to put it in their own jargon. Not an ordinary case, but a case of cold-blooded murder or assassination. According to the criminal code which they memorized from the beginning of their police career, if they were found guilty, they would be hanged. Yet they were not bothered. At night they behaved like newly married couples on a honeymoon, laughing, watching x-rated movies, and making love as much of the night as they could possibly convert to their use.

At five o'clock as their alarm clocks rang, Prison Superintendent Fakade revved his Peugeot 505 engine to signal for Private Oyibo and Corporal Shegbe to come to enter the car for the five-mile trip to Warri Central Prison, known in town as Okere High College. The fence was so high that Superintendent Fakade, like his predecessors, always boasted that no convict had ever escaped from it. Those outside did not know what transpired inside but occasionally saw the less dangerous and poor prisoners clearing grass outside and singing worksongs.

Warri Central Prison was the only prison in Warri, so nobody knew why it had been named Central. It was the prison in which people convicted of crimes in the entire old Delta province were kept. There were hundreds of police stations, hundreds of magistrate and high courts, but only one prison. It was monstrous in size and parents threatened troublesome children with sending them to Okere High College. It might be that the original planners wanted to build smaller prisons in the Oil City but the proverbial lack of government funds after programmes were announced might have shut off the plan's implementation. Also the underhand freedom of generous convicts and suspects did not make more prisons necessary. The police and prison authorities prospered from one big central prison, where the unconnected and poor prisoner was likely to die as an inmate or come out fatally diseased.

The policemen came out of the car and followed the Prison Superintendent to their nearby "cells," two rooms attached to that wing of cells. The two rooms used to be offices of warders, who had been given new offices. The vacant rooms, now called "cells," were rented out to important prisoners, those who could buy privileges in Superintendent Fakade's kingdom. Rich inmates wanted to leave prison after completing their sentences alive and that would not be possible if they were kept in the regular cells where mistreatment and strange infectious diseases condemned them to almost definite death.

Private Oyibo and Corporal Shegbe were well dressed, perfumed, and looked far better than policemen of their ranks who were usually poorly and irregularly paid. But Private Oyibo was not a mere private, nor Corporal Shegbe a mere corporal.

"Man pass man," prison guards and officials always told poor convicts or detainees who complained but did not have the financial wherewithal to relieve their inhuman conditions.

"So you no go help?" some prisoners would ask in a pleading tone.

"Money for hand," the prison officials would answer.

The prisoners understood the language. They could not be given preferential treatment until they gave out money. Money for hand, back for ground. It was the lingo of prostitutes in Okoye Street which has spread, and has been picked up by the Shylocks and those who avoid helping others without making demands for financial remuneration.

* * *

The Prison Superintendent himself had brought from the car two Thermos "coolers" of jollof rice and fried chicken, which the police detainees would take for lunch. They took their breakfast very early, just before they were picked and had late dinners at the guest-house with their wives. They said they could not take the prison's half-cooked beans and garri twice a day. Mrs. Fakade was the food contractor for Warri Central Prison and was doing very well as far as business was concerned. That meant she was starving the inmates to make maximum profit. She kept much of her money to herself, knowing that should her rich husband die by chance before her, his relatives would seize all his wealth and leave her with nothing. She saw herself as planning for tomorrow.

Superintendent Fakade acted as a public relations officer for his fee-paying prisoners. A week earlier he had told the press that the two policemen were on hunger strike for being falsely accused of a murder they did not and could not have committed. However, he said everything was under control and he would use any means, short of physically breaking their backs but including force if persuasion failed, to make them eat before the trial began. In *The Daily Times*, a report appeared about their harsh treatment, being mixed with convicts and being given food not fit for human consumption, despite the fact that they were only suspects and theirs could be wrongful arrest and detention. Mr. Fakade projected the image of a tough prison superintendent that the military government loved and he was bent on self-promotion to accelerate his professional advancement. That many convicts died in his prison was taken by the government as a good sign. Better not go into Superintendent Fakade's jail if you love your life. His public relations job was very successful.

At ten o'clock at night, whatever the weather, Superintendent Fakade personally came to take the two men to his car parked by his office, having dismissed his personal driver for the day. He felt this was not what he could entrust to any other hand. Not because he would have to pay much for the help, but in this work you did not want to let everybody into secret commitments. He had to take them to his guest-house at ten and bring them back to Warri Central Prison at five. He had to be careful, even though he was the overall boss. By the time he retired in two or three years, he would be rich enough not to rely on his pension. Who can live on a paltry pension that inflation reduces to nothing? he asked himself. These two detainees, suspects, prisoners, or whatever their status, have contributed immensely to his wealth and he would fulfill his part of the unwritten contract.

In Private Oyibo and Corporal Shegbe he was paying back the police in their own coin. The police, judges, and other court officials got bribes and they, prison officials, were meant to keep those who had been milked dry to wait for their deaths. He would not mind stealing from a robber much of what the robber had taken from others. That was the way he saw his pact with the two policemen.

Still Prison Superintendent Fakade wondered how two very low-ranking policemen were able to muster the huge amount of *kola* they gave to him to help them. Who could give out such a huge amount to be taken care of in jail must have so much more in reserve for the actual court case, he felt. As the prison's boss, he was in a position to help, more so with the incentive of boxes of naira he had never seen with people he considered poor. What is a private or corporal in the police? Close to office messenger, he retorted in his mind. Now he could understand why Alhaji Lawal, his retired predecessor in the office, had sent him a congratulatory card on his appointment, handwriting "You have made it. You are in charge of a gold mine. Make the best of it till you retire, Debo." For his part, Alhaji Lawal started a major transportation company, and his Peugeot 504 cars and Mercedes buses crisscrossed the country, piling up money for the retired prison boss who called himself the people's alhaji.

Mr. Debo Fakade was already a little rich but wanted to be counted among the naira-blessed nationwide. They were not many in that exclusive club bur he wanted to be one of the select few. He was already ascending the great heights of wealth and he could see a range of mountains ahead of him. It took energy, courage, and focus to be at the top, he told himself.

His senior son at Hussey College had almost embarrassed him but the matter was promptly suppressed. Imagine if the nosy dailies or weeklies carried the news of a prison superintendent's son playing Robin Hood at school. That was what his son had done, stolen his money to give to a poor classmate. His son had taken what others called plenty of money, but which he didn't even notice, to give to his needy classmate. Their class master got to know about it and sent for him. Of course, the bastard of a teacher wanted some money and he had enough to shut his mouth tight. What he considered a pittance more than pleased the teacher.

Superintendent Fakade only worried about armed robbers, with his son revealing that he did not keep his money in the bank. Who keeps money nowadays in banks which tomorrow will get distressed? I had thought only human beings get distressed; now it is also banks, he mused. Why keep money in banks when a mad military officer could freeze your accounts? If governors converted their state houses to safes and do not go to the bank, why should other people be fooled to bank money? My money should always be within my reach, he told himself then.

Superintendent Fakade could not trust students and teachers. Many of them were in jail serving long sentences, that is, when they are not executed for robbery. The evidence was in Warri Central Prison. But he had so vehemently denied before the stupid teacher that he had so many cartons of money in closets and the unused rooms in his big house.

The trial date had been set for the following week and the two murder suspects would appear to prove their innocence. Technically, that was what they were until proved otherwise, that is, guilty. Nobody had caught them red-handed, but they had been seen by many regular travellers of that road who had been held hostage until they paid a ransom of naira to be allowed to pass.

Private Oyibo and Corporal Shegbe awaited trial for the murder of Superintendent of Police, Mr. Egbe. The police superintendent in mufti had been gunned down and his car with his bullet-perforated body abandoned beside an unauthorized roadblock. Private Oyibo and Corporal Shegbe have insisted that there was no way they could mount a roadblock without authorization and were at their desks at the time ascribed to the killing of Mr. Egbe. They knew what alibi was; and wanted to use it as one of their many defence strategies.

As members of the Nigerian Police, they knew the public knew that senior officers sent privates and corporals to the road to extort money from travellers and make returns to them at the end of the day or week. Nobody even in the police force would believe that such low-ranking men would have the audacity to mount a roadblock for months without a higher authority behind them. Apart from the police chief himself, who else knew their roadblock was illegal? They could imagine the people already suspecting they were sent by Mr. Egbe himself. They knew the public did not trust the police, that the people did not trust their brothers, uncles, or relatives in the police force whose known tactic was exaggerating a problem in order to extract maximum bribes.

As for the court, money would win the case. They would give a clean used Peugeot 504 to the judge's wife for her shopping. The judge would know what to do--dismiss the case. There was precedence in this. A retired topmost government official gave a Mercedes Benz to a judge's wife and the judge dutifully squashed the case. That was the end of the matter with the embattled retired official. Money is power. Money can buy justice in Nigeria. Almost every government worker was hungry for money. A dog with its mouth full cannot bark. As for the private and the corporal, they had made enough money that could save them from jail or hanging. Already the Prison Superintendent was on their side, his mouth full, and he had been sent to the trial judge, Mr. Justice Isaiah Okitikpi, with big envelopes of money. The car would be sent to him later.

The two policemen did not feel remorse for what they had been accused of. They felt they had to kill, if they did not want to be jailed for life or killed. After all, Mr. Egbe by implication would say they were armed robbers. If you had guns and stopped travellers and demanded that they must buy their passage through your roadblock where you were not authorized to be, was that not armed robbery? they had reasoned. The punishment for convicted armed robbers was execution by firing squad or hanging watched by a crowd in an open field. And there had been many armed robbers in police or military uniform. What they were experiencing now was very temporary. They have sworn to deny killing Mr. Egbe, though they rejoiced at clearing an obstacle from their way. They had already made so much money from the roadblock that once released, they would still have more than enough money to live luxuriously the lives of three tortoises combined.

Mr. Egbe, the murdered Superintendent of Police, liked taking the short-cut. He preferred taking the Warri-Ekakpamre road to Ughelli. That road was never busy and drivers with license or insurance problems took it to avoid three roadblocks on the Warri-Agbarho-Ughelli road, part of the busy Port Harcourt-Lagos road. At the roadblock before Agbarho there could be a long line of cars and one could waste thirty minutes or more, even if the police passed you without search or questioning. There was no way of driving through other cars in front. However, on the freer shortcut road, travellers feared armed robbers who frequently operated on it, especially after sundown.

On one of his frequent private trips to Ughelli after office hours, Superintendent of Police, Joseph Egbe, had been stopped or rather had to stop at a roadblock he knew very well he or any in the Warri Police Command had not authorized. He had many cars, some as gifts; this time he was using his wife's Honda Accord. He saw the private and corporal doing their tollgate collection of naira from drivers and motor cyclists going either way. He came down and, of course, the two policemen recognized their big boss. They were not working directly under him at the headquarters, but they recognized him from the parade ground, his photographs which they had seen many times, and from a distance while he went about his duties in and out of police administrative offices.

"Good evening, sir," they saluted.

"Good evening," he replied.

They looked at each other for a few seconds in which the two junior policemen knew they were in big trouble.

"What are you both doing here at this time?" the police chief asked.

"Nothing, sir, just directing traffic," Corporal Shegbe replied.

"Shut up!" he shouted.

"Yes, sir," the two replied standing at attention with their guns pointed sideways from Mr. Egbe.

"Who sent you here?" he again asked.

"Nobody, sir," they replied.

"What do you mean by 'Nobody'? Do you tell me you came here on your own?"

"Yes, sir."

"Remove this roadblock and never you come here again," he ordered.

"Agreed, sir," they answered.

"Leave immediately!"

"Thanks, sir."

Joseph Egbe, SP, was surprised only two weeks later when passing the same way he saw both Private Oyibo and Corporal Shegbe again manning the same unofficial roadblock. He was driving another car, so there was no way the two policemen could recognize him until he stopped and came out. He gave them what he termed a final warning, a serious reprimand, and threatened them not only with dismissal but the rest of their lives in jail if he found them again manning an illegal roadblock. The warning was clear and harsh and they hurriedly dismantled the roadblock in his presence and left.

Barely ten days after this incident, SP Joseph Egbe felt his verbal reprimand had had the desired effect of curtailing some of the excesses of the force. He didn't want to be high-handed; otherwise, he could dismiss the private and the corporal who were just small fish in police waters. As an insider he knew what top officers, including the Head of Police, did with bribes. It was always better to warn and warn subordinates before taking harsh measures which could destroy their careers. Khaki no be leather, they say in pidgin, he told himself. It's hard for the ones at the bottom, he knew. The boss in the force had so much power over subordinates but that power must be exercised prudently. It is like a weapon put in your hands, which you don't have to abuse. He remembered what his Ghanaian friend used to tell him. Power is like an egg--hold it too tightly and it breaks, hold it loosely and it will fall and break. He tried to maintain a certain balance and he was happy the corporal and private had apologised and heeded his warning by dismantling the roadblock in his very presence before he continued his journey.

As he cruised on the fairly lonely road, his thoughts were on his concubine who had promised him *banga* soup with bitter leaf and fresh fish, what he considered the best food to round off the working week. His Mercedes sped while he anticipated the night with Omare, a woman who knew how to make a man happy. Then as he turned at the only corner in the rather straight road, he saw a few people ahead with two drums and a stick stuck with nails across the road. He had already passed the spot where the private and the corporal had mounted their roadblock the two times he caught them. His mind flew to armed robbers. He had not carried his revolver because Omare had told him in an earlier visit that fear of his gun around prevented her from having an orgasm. However, he had the charm against robbers made for him by one of the best known medicine-men in the area. He was not afraid of robbers.

He suddenly pressed down his brakes and the car came to a screeching stop. Though ruffled, he immediately regained his composure. He then realized the two men were in police uniform. Still Private Oyibo and Corporal Shegbe blocking the road. They had moved further down the road than the two times he had found them.

SP Egbe was highly enraged and knew he had to teach the recalcitrant policemen an unforgettable lesson. Some men, he told himself, invite destruction upon themselves. He has had enough. As he came out, the two policemen panicked and almost wanted to run away. But they calmed down almost immediately and remembered the oath they had taken and the plan of action they had made in the event that they were disturbed again by Mr. Egbe. They looked at each other for a split second and fired their already cocked rifles at the target moving towards them. Corporal Shegbe fired thrice at his head, Private Oyibo thrice at his chest.

"Why disturb us? Poor man no go chop?" Private Oyibo shouted at the slumping body.

"How you buy your cars? Na government loan or from your salary? You don't want poor man to drink garri, fool," Corporal Shegbe declaimed before the body on the ground.

The two motorists who had been stopped at the illegal roadblock before Superintendent Egbe's arrival jumped into their cars and continued their trip to wherever they were going, shaking and almost running into the bush. Who wants to be a police witness? Crown witness? Drivers saw the body and the blood-spattered patch of the road, but who wanted to be the police witness and be falsely accused of the murder by the same police either to cover their ineptitude or satisfy their greed for bribery? Afraid, nobody stopped to help the mortally wounded Superintendent Egbe and he soon bled to death.

Though their action had been carefully planned, Private Oyibo and Corporal Shegbe threw their guns down and ran away. SP Joseph Egbe's corpse and two guns lay on the ground on the roadside for police to take to Warri the following day after news of his death had spread all over town.

"Oh these armed robbers must be heartless," some cried out.

"I don't know, but police work too dangerous," others said.

"Some police collude with them and share the booty," some other people commented.

"Na so life be. He don go," an old man commented.

The Warri Police High Command sent out word nationwide to search for the culprits of this dastard murder. They could not identify the two guns found beside their superintendent's body. There was no good record of guns in the command and they did not want to expose their inefficiency. They declared that the guns and perhaps the robbers must have come from another state. The police guarding the Niger Bridge before Onitsha were told to carefully search cars and people going to the East. At Oluku Junction at the outskirts of Benin, the police were ordered to stop and check carefully cars going towards Lagos.

No suspect was in police hands until SSP Osaye was sent from Lagos to help track the culprits. He had wanted the fingerprint expert in Lagos to come and assist in determining who had the guns, but their tools were limited and they would thus be of no use, especially without any suspects held. But SSP Osaye pursued the case with a group of Criminal Investigation Department officials who under cover asked questions from motor parks and markets to beer parlours and stumbled upon important leads which made them to focus on members of the police force in Warri.

Within ten days of SSP Osaye's take-over of the case, the investigation started to yield positive results. From the description of those who had passed the roadblock, police detectives gradually zeroed in on their own men who were strangely enough now showing up in their Igbudu Police Station which had been inoperational for over six months. SSP Osaye wondered why it took so long to have them arrested. The two men were picked from their homes in Warri one early morning after being observed for several days. The arrests were reported in the national dailies and SSP Osaye was praised for his diligence.

The trial was three days away. The police were ready with the prosecution, the suspects ready with Barrister Igbi, London-trained, to defend them. PS Fakade had worked with the attorney and the judge on behalf of both Private Oyibo and Corporal Shegbe. When he dropped them at the guest-house on Saturday night, they discussed the defence strategy and were all satisfied about the state of things. Things looked great. The police suspects felt they had prepared themselves for war and they were confident of victory.

Two nights to the trial day, Private Oyibo and Corporal Shegbe won a big prize. The gate-man and gardener, a prisoner in Mr. Fakade's personal assignment, had teased the two suspects several times the last three weeks on why they didn't attempt to escape.

"If I be you, I for run commot here," he told them as they came to his post to chat with him one night.

"Why have you not run away yourself?" Corporal Shegbe asked him.

"Wetin I go run for? If I run, I no go enjoy as I de do for here," he told them.

The two men got the message but they had to be wary of this type of unsolicited advice from their guard. He must have been planted there by PS Fakade to be his eye on them. The reasoning was right though. A poor but well-treated prisoner didn't need to escape to a worse plight, but they had much to lose, bearing in mind how much they had outside. True, they had sought and got the cooperation of Mr. Fakade and through him the trial judge whom they had promised an enviable gift. But for all their preparations, a court case could always spring a surprise, depending on the circumstances. Mr. Egbe's family and the Warri Police Command should not be underestimated in how far they would go to commit money and other resources to the trial too. And of course, Judge Isaiah Okitikpi was not only a tortoise like his kind but also a Government-appointee and could dance to the music of the Government. In that case, he might not be swayed by bribes alone.

After the two police suspects assured themselves that the gate-man, Raymond Olotu, was not a spy, they decided to pursue the arrangement. They were aware of many suspects who escaped and had not been found. Even in cases of some bloody abortive coups, the Federal Government with its two hundred thousand army and forty thousand police force failed to arrest the escapee officers. Most of such wanted people slipped through their fingers, either hidden in the country or escaped through the borders with other army or policemen escorting them.

The strategy session for the escape plan had been finalised. Everything must go on as usual to avoid any suspicion. The greatest advantage in war is a surprise attack and they had to exploit this advantage to its maximum. Their wives would go with them. They would take off as soon as Prisons Superintendent dropped them at about 10.20 p.m. and left for his own house. They would use a close relative's car and be dropped in Corporal Shegbe's cousin's hamlet deep in Ife farmlands. Akpona had gone to his Ife bush village for over twenty years, and for the first ten years his whereabouts were unknown. After he was believed dead, he showed up to everybody's surprise on the first day of Eni Festival and had visited home two other times and always at festivals. Corporal Shegbe had gone there five years earlier and stayed with Akpona, his wife, and three children in their farm. He had wondered then what could drive a man to live that kind of life. By then he had not heard the story that Akpona had eloped with somebody else's wife. The few times he had visited home, his wife had not accompanied him. Akpona went once or twice a month to the market at Modakeke where nobody knew him. He was a man on his own and was as unknown in his homeplace as in his migrant home.

When Mr. Fakade arrived at 5 a.m. on Sunday, the day before the trial would begin, he observed the gate already thrown open. The lights in the chalets were ablaze. He revved his car engine as usual. He heard some loud pig-like grunting and, looking into that direction, saw his prisoner-help on the ground. He came down and saw his hands and legs bound tight. In a well-rehearsed gasping voice, he told Mr. Fakade of being attacked by a group who later also bound Private Oyibo, Corporal Shegbe, and their wives and drove them away in a landrover.

"The men come as if na you send them to come remove furniture from the unused chalets and before I fit ask for who them be, they don slap me 'Kpai' many times and before lightning flash they throw me for ground and tie my hands and legs. They say if I shout, they go shoot me, so I shut my mouth *jeje*," he narrated to his boss.

This was not a story that Prisons Superintendent Fakade could tell the court or the world. He was used to self-advertising public relations. He knew he had to do a lot of damage control and suppression of evidence to get off the hook. He quickly removed his gate-man to his rightful place in one of the worst cells in the prison. How was he going to deal with presenting the two accused to the court? What would he say happened to them in Warri Central Prison? He put his mind to work a strategy to tear himself out of a net.

When he drove to Warri Central Prison to inform the warders to bring out Private Oyibo and Corporal Shegbe from their cells, he knew he had a big challenge ahead for him. The warders knew that he knew that they knew what had been happening. These warders who had felt short-changed by their boss openly grumbled that he had let the two accused out for a big prize. They had been bypassed and were never allowed to be anywhere near those people they were supposed to keep watch over in the prison. Once in a while the other prisoners or suspects gave them tips that helped them meet their personal financial demands. They felt Mr. Fakade wanted only himself to "chop" and had abandoned them to starve.

"Wetin 'im still want sef? Why he de snatch food from our mouth?" they questioned themselves.

They were ready to testify in court to absolve themselves from blame for the disappearance of the two police suspects. They would openly tell the court that the two men were kept at Prisons Superintendent's guest-house and not in jail. The best kept open secret would now be divulged.

Prisons Superintendent Fakade knew very well the consequences should his dissatisfied subordinates appear in the trial court. He used diplomacy and money to shut talkative mouths. As long as nobody challenged him in court, whatever they said behind him did not matter. Nobody ever dared to insult the Oba face-to-face. The promotion, accelerated promotion, and confirmation exercise was ahead and he promised his subordinates individually the strongest recommendation possible. He knew the right bait to throw before his gullible workers and they swallowed it worm, hook, and thread. Those who are desperate go for any promise dangled before them. The promise of a few hundred naira took care of what Mr. Fakade described as the troublesome home front.

The case was not called that Monday but delayed till Friday. Whether Judge Okitikpi had heard murmurings of the disappearance or kidnapping of Private Oyibo and Corporal Shegbe, nobody in court except Prisons Superintendent Fakade could tell. In the interim Mr. Fakade fine-tuned his strategy, oiled his weapon, as he put it, to win the battle without bloodshed. He called a press conference of selected journalists and told his favoured members of the press that a group scaled the impossible prison walls to abduct the two missing accused policemen.

On Friday the case was called. The prosecution did not show up. Within ten minutes the assassination case was over. Judge Isaiah Okitikpi threw out the case as there was no prosecution and Government could not produce the accused. Mr. Fakade felt relieved that the judge had kept his side of the bargain to take care of the prosecution. With the prosecuting dogs overfed, they might have fallen into a three-day slumber from which they would not wake till after the case was over!

Before the promotion exercise began, Mr. Fakade sent a letter to Lagos giving three months' notice of his intention to retire. Sent to the Federal Department of Prisons, none of his workers in Warri knew about his plan. He wanted, according to him, to leave the dance while he was still being applauded. He saw ahead a comfortable retirement life in Lagos after a pilgrimage to Jerusalem, which would make him "Retired Prisons Superintendent Debo Fakade, JP." Upon his return from the Holy Land, he would have a thanksgiving service at St. James Church and a retirement party that evening to conclude his prisons' career. He felt he had made it, only after going through the eye of the Nigerian Needle.

the major's appeal

I believed till the news came that my friend's life would be spared. It is true he fired the gun but he didn't aim it at anybody. Efe wanted to shoot only into the air to scare off a village mob he knew would wreak havoc and cause many deaths. But as things would go that day, the very instance he was pulling the trigger, he was pushed from the back by a member of the rival family. That jostle or push made what was aimed at the sky to fly lower than expected and the consequence was fatal. The major's rifle was loaded. Nobody was more scared than Major Efe Segine himself over the bloodshed. Nobody was more appalled than he.

But what were second thoughts when the fated have been pushed beyond their contemplated aims? Witnesses and the court would ignore the efforts he made to save Akoro's life. He carried the bleeding man into his car, himself totally bloodstained. But he hadn't taken off for hospital before the man died. There had been pandemonium, but Akoro's people knew that their man had been shot dead. They dragged out his body like an army retrieving its dead for decent burial and soon Efe's uncle's compound was in flames. While there was a death followed by an act of arson that consumed a car and a house, it was only the death that became the court case. Efe's people felt it would be too insensitive for them to complain about a burnt house and a car when the other side suffered a human loss. Sometimes, you have to be sensitive to your enemy's feelings.

To the judge Efe had a gun and he, not anybody else, pulled the trigger. My friend did not deny that he fired. It was not an ill-gotten weapon. It was an Army rifle assigned to my friend, not a dane gun. According to the judge, even if a spoon or spade spat fire and killed, the wielder of the weapon was guilty of murder. The criminal code is explicit on this, he said in his comments.

* * *

Major Segine had decided at the last moment to drive rather than fly from Lagos to Enugu for the Army's public relations officers' conference. He was driving not because he was scared of military plane crashes which were frequent, but he wanted to seize the opportunity of attending the conference to see his family and people at Okpara before heading for Enugu. Okpara was about midway between Lagos and Enugu. He had rarely seen his people ever since he was transferred from Kaduna. He had felt that when in Lagos he would visit home more often, but he soon learnt like many workers in Lagos that there was something in the city that pulled you in but hardly let you out when you wanted to leave. He visited home twice a year while in Kaduna. He had been in Lagos for a year and had not had the time or opportunity to visit Okpara once.

But that decision to drive and not to fly with his colleagues in an airforce plane was to drastically change and end his life. How could he know in his desire to visit home after a long absence that he was following the path of death? Of course, if he foresaw death on his way, he would definitely have taken a different course. But that is life, that the future is impenetrable.

He would survive the potholed roads littered with metal scraps of victims' cars that Ogun lured into fatalities. He survived armed robbers who no longer wore masks or hid their identities to rob. He survived the police whose frequent roadblocks at awkward parts of the road caused fatal accidents. He survived the crazy drivers who flew cars and drove the Lagos-Warri road twice or thrice daily. But he would fare differently in his hometown.

Okpara elders say that the town elevates you only to crash you down. The town, elders also say, is very slippery in the dry season. Major Efe Segine was coming in February when it hardly rained and the harmattan winds battered people and trees. Rubber tappers were happy because the trees produced more latex than usual in the cold season. The people knew that the harmattan was the remote harbinger of the hot season. After cold, heat!

My friend drove into town in the late afternoon. By this time those who went to farms or to tap rubber were back at home. We who were born and grew up in Okpara had known it to be divided by one issue or another. Our friendship survived the divisions. Once upon a time you were for either the Cock or the Palm Tree, symbols of Zik's NCNC and Awo's AG. You would think that these were not just political parties but family associations. Their Opiri Dance Troupe split into two competing groups and their fame went down. They went in and out of court because of land cases. Of course, the lawyers in Warri and Sapele prospered at their expense.

In recent years there had been problems about a new market. There was no common ground and up till today there are two competing markets in town, none a match for the neighbouring Kokori market which is big and draws buyers and sellers from far and near. And when it came to building a secondary school, they had two instead of one. There is a Catholic one at the Isiokoro end of town and an Anglican one at the Omwe River end of town. It did not matter to the people that the two schools could have pulled together resources for one with more students, a bigger library, and a better furnished laboratory than the empty rooms they had for them in each of the schools.

Major Segine came to town in February when the harmattan winds were flaring nerves of competing factions. Supporters of two national parties were at each other's throat before the Presidential election. The Segines were descendants of Saduwa who had been a prosperous and very important chief. Whether there was truth in it or not, I don't know. But he was said to be an alien, from Benin; and up till today the saying continues, "Saduwa may be rich but he remains an alien." Whether that was said to spite a powerful chief who humiliated many Okpara men and women, I don't know. Saduwa's father or mother must have been an Okpara-born, but that fact has been lost in distortions and deep family prejudices. In Okpara the rational was abandoned when it came to factional rivalry.

My father and the other Tebus belong to the Uvo family, self-proclaimed descendants of giants. Uvo was a warrior giant who defended Okpara when invaded by neighbouring clans. My father told me what we did not say in public, that Uvo raided neighbouring villages at will and looted and wreaked havoc in most of them. What is important to us as a family is Uvo's heroism. We are a family of giants. My father, by the way, is a very smallish man and has not imbibed the giant genes of his great ancestor.

The evening my friend Major Segine arrived, as custom demands of him, he left his car in his father's compound and set out on foot to go from house to house to greet his relations and neighbours. He usually went beyond his Saduwa section into ours because many of us in Okpara despite the legendary rivalry of the two big families were friends. My friendship with Efe was not a rare thing in Okpara. Efe came to his uncle's compound at the very moment the Uvo family activists of CPN came to clash with the Saduwa supporters of NUP. It was his attempt to scare off the dangerous mob, his attempt to douse the fires of destruction, that was deflected to kill the CPN's spokesman. It was as if a fatal ambush had been set for him and he walked into it with open eyes. He did not regret his intention till the end, for he insisted even in the playhouse that was the court that it was the soldier's first instinct to protect lives and not to kill.

* * *

I visited my friend after he was condemned to death but was aware of attempts to secure clemency for him. He was still his calm old self, a hundred percent sure that he would get out of this hole of a problem as he had gone out of earlier ones. By then the civilian government elected in chaos had been overthrown by the military.

"Will the military allow its own to be executed because of a bloody civilian killed accidentally?" he asked.

"Chances are far better now that Army boys are in power," I told him.

"They have the power to protect their own," he as an insider told me.

"We are praying and working on it relentlessly," I said.

A major used to be a powerful officer in the army during the civil war. But the war had been over for over a decade and rapid promotions of all who had carried guns had made meaningless many ranks like captain and major. Many junior officers had things their own way with civilians, since they knew that they, the military, were in power. To curb the excesses of looting, rape, and wanton indiscipline of his soldiers, General Dudu had reined in his boys. No nonsense. Do any nonsense and get court martialed. There is nothing more terrifying for the military than being court martialed.

When CPN won the local and federal elections, its Okpara supporters who were opponents of the Segine family had the police re-write the report, as I was to learn too late. The case was tried in a court whose judge was a CPN partisan. The Uvo family and CPN members in town wanted to show that there was another power stronger than the gun, they wanted to show the Saduwas and their relatives, the Segines, that they would defeat them in the case by having their most illustrious son not only condemned but executed by hanging for murder. They wanted to inflict the ultimate shame on their enemies. All the generations of animosity coalesced into one case that had to be won at all cost. Each side visited diviners and medicine-men, each side taxed itself financially to influence the police. But court cases had their own ways of ending in the state.

My father had sought my support in vain in earlier factional issues like the market and secondary school locations. Sometimes I supported my family, at other times I was against them. Our people have a proverb that one's relation is special. They also say that blood is thicker than water. However, I never believed and still do not believe that one's sense of right or wrong should be conditioned by family relationship. The market should be built in a central place in town and the first secondary school built should remain and be expanded, I told my father.

"You modern ones don't know what family honour means," he told me.

"We should do what is good for all Okpara people," I said.

So when my friend's case came, he understood his duty as my father. He did not follow the family to court, nor did he contribute any money, insisting that he had no money. However, I wanted him to do more for me to help my friend. I asked him to help stop the litigation at the beginning but he said it was beyond him. He could be driven from his compound and tagged a traitor by his own people. It was easier, he told me, for me his son to be neutral or support my friend than for himself who was deep in the traditional rivalry. He said he would tactfully discourage them, but whatever he did discreetly did not work.

Litigation leads to ever more serious and uncharted troubles. When I heard of the case in Warri, I thought it was something that could be disposed of fairly quickly. My Major friend was not an armed robber. An accident in the midst of a political clash was simply an accidental discharge that should be treated as such. But I was to be proved wrong in this as in other expectations of sanity in the court system. But I am not blaming only the court and the judicial system. Nor do I blame my friend's fate solely on the Uvo family who went to court with vengeance. Maybe that was what they had to do at their level of consciousness. Nor do I blame my friend for his humane intentions of trying to avert mob violence. Many could hold a lamp in daylight and still fall into a pit, I have learnt.

When I visited my friend in Benin where he had been transferred after his conviction, he was more excited and hopeful of his immediate release. The trial was a plaything that bewildered both sides. Its swiftness and the blatant bias of the judge should have been good grounds for appeal in a murder case, but appeals for murder cases had been ruled out because of frequent armed robberies.

However, there was hope now that the court verdict would be repudiated in one way or another with time. Fortunately, at least in our optimism, Efe's senior at Federal Government College, Warri, Colonel Fawole was Governor of Bendel State. Olu Fawole graduated from the school just before Efe entered, but they had met. Alumni of the same college and both in the Army. What a happy coincidence! Other alumni, friends, and Efe's family had managed to reach the Governor and told him of the case, its trial, and verdict. He understood that he was the last hope for Efe's acquittal and he promised to act on it favourably. Colonel Fawole then instructed the case's file to be brought and the application for executive clemency be submitted.

The file moved slowly from Warri to Benin through the police commands and court registrars and arrived on the Governor's table among a heap of miscellaneous files for signature. There were certificates of occupancy, contracts, and several completed applications for executive clemency. Subordinates tried to smuggle in many files from families and persons they had received huge bribes to push their cases before the Governor. The Governor's signature was state law that many civil servants and orderlies exploited to become rich.

If Colonel Fawole had gone to the office for another week, my friend would be alive today. His signature was needed to save his life. But there are many things beyond our control. Even the best scheduled tasks are prone to unexpected changes. A week is a long time in Nigeria, with frequent changes of weather.

The Uvo camp at Okpara had their own monitors who eavesdropped into what they called the "plot" to deceive the Governor to free a murderer. Apart from delaying the file on its way to Benin, they made noise about it to Colonel Fawole's hearing. Maybe to President Dudu's hearing too. The Uvos sowed rumours which soon sprouted and grew tall for everybody to see. They said that the Governor had been given millions of naira to free Major Segine. Nobody asked who in the Saduwa family could raise that fantastic amount, but merely mentioning a million naira was enough for a hand about to sign a colleague off death row to think twice of his action and its possible repercussion on his own career. The survival instinct was strong. There was no time for Colonel Fawole to hold the pen and attempt to sign Efe's clemency.

The history of a nation could run contrary to notions of individual justice. President Dudu, in his strategy to involve as many officers as possible in governance and not to leave any of his state governors too long in a location, frequently reassigned his officers. This, he thought, would also solidify his presidency. In this exercise, Colonel Fawole was posted to Defence Headquarters with immediate effect. In his place Colonel Dong swiftly took over.

Colonel Dong was welcomed to his office with petitions

from many parts of the state. From the look of these petitions, one would feel that Colonel Fawole merely sat on his governor's seat from eight to four without attending to the problems of the state. It seemed nothing moved forward all the time he was in Benin. The Uvo family petition was one of the strongest and raised threats of bringing in the press if any *wuru-wuru* or hanky-panky was done to grant clemency to a convicted murderer. The state was notorious for petitions and backbiting but this inflammatory spate was unusual. Colonel Dong felt he had to tread softly with this problem.

As an army man, the military governor felt he was walking in a minefield and he had to look out carefully to advance, and needed to clear the fields of danger first before doing anything else. Petitions in states had been the undoing of many past governors. He did not know what those petitions were about and did not want to be bogged down by petitions. How long were you a governor in a military regime that you had to spend all your time answering complaints? He took the easiest way through the minefield ahead of him, a digression that bypassed danger. He ordered all pending parole, reprieve, and clemency cases thrown away. Let the courts settle their cases, he said.

I visited my friend again in his cell in Benin Federal Prisons. Two warders who did me a favor after I explained my friendship with ex-Major Segine followed me and stood in full view, though were polite enough to ignore our conversation. My friend did not show he was disturbed by events, maybe because he had not heard of his case like others for clemency thrown out. He had not heard but he should have known within him that the Army had discharged him without benefits. That was the practice of the Army--abandoning its own once perceived to be tainted. In this case, none checked the veracity or circumstances of the first-degree murder verdict.

I told him what no other person would tell him. I felt even if he was to die, he should not die without a memory. There had been some bad news, which I felt would relieve him rather

than break him. Efe was a man of indefatigable hope. His life
so far had shown that.

"There's been a death at home," I told him.

"Who?" he asked.

"Your junior sister," I said.

He gnashed his teeth and gestured as if he was helpless. I
decided to tell him what had happened, so that he would not
grieve in vain. He had always felt that out of all his brothers
and sisters, this one was closest to him and she had visited him
wherever he had been posted in the army.

"She fell sick suddenly of a fever. You know fevers are
common ailments at home, so common that nobody fears
falling sick of malaria. But hers was a strange case from the
beginning. She couldn't move or eat and became hysterical.
When your family wanted to take her to Eku Baptist Hospital,
she refused and said she would certainly die if she entered the
hospital yard.

'I have done something,' she confessed.

'What?' they asked her.

'I can't say it,' she said.

Everybody was surprised. After much coaxing in which she
was promised prayers by elders for her recovery if she told the
truth, she admitted what everybody expected she would say in
those circumstances.

'I'm a witch,' she blurted out.

Your people knew that was not all. You know our people,
they feel almost every woman is a witch and so being a witch
itself was not enough for her to fear dying from simple malaria
if she had not done anything evil.

'We are listening,' they told her, 'Go on.'

Then she dropped the bombshell that stunned all your
family people who have been going through very hard times
because of this your case.

'I have been trying to kill Efe,' she told them.

Our people know that a witch does not confess everything

at once and felt she had not told the most terrible part of her plot. They believed there was much more to say.

'I'm the one who made Efe's case impossible to win. There will be no clemency for him. I hid the file here and there and that was why it did not get to Benin in time. Now I threw it away so that nobody in the Governor's seat will ever see it to sign. Since you told me to say everything, I have to say this. He's already slaughtered, and we have shared him for a big party in the coven,' she told a family dumbfounded and stung with pain and shame.

'What can be done to reverse the case?' they asked her in a threatening manner.

She was no longer ashamed, nor was she afraid of whatever the family would do to her. She cared for no consequence at that stage.

'It's too late. I submitted him as my contribution to a festival and the food is already consumed,' she told them.

She was abandoned by the family and we heard she died the following day. The earth does not reject any corpse and she was buried in the bush and nobody will ever know where she was buried."

Efe closed his eyes, inhaled and exhaled. He appeared relieved. He reminded me of his experience when an undergraduate.

"Do you still remember that I was almost expelled from the University? I had travelled to Warri, in fact, to see Titi now dead. She had a problem with her husband and I felt my sister should not be treated like a slave by anybody and went to show that she was not alone but from a family that cared. When I was away, there was a student riot. Benin was like a battle-ground that day. Federal and state cars were vandalized, many burnt; a few buildings were torched. Some university officials were kidnapped but released. The Vice Chancellor's residence was burnt to the ground. When I heard of it from the radio, I felt lucky that I was not there because I heard that many innocent passersby had their cars destroyed and many sustained severe injuries.

As I came back late in the evening, I was picked by the police as the leader of the student rioters who committed the destruction in the campus and city. Nobody at first believed me despite my swearing that I was away and had no knowledge of the plan to demonstrate. I lost a semester instead of being expelled, only after they half-believed me," he reminisced.

"Of course, I knew about it," I told him.

"I shall be free," he said as if talking to himself rather than me.

The warders signalled that I had to leave and I left with the feeling that my friend had accepted his fate. He had tried to live right and wondered why things had gone very wrong on several occasions. His last question then was, "Could Titi do what she said she did?" I didn't answer the question as the warders physically pulled me away. Up till today, I don't know whether I can answer that question.

The last time I visited him, it appeared he had heard or instinctively learnt about his situation. In fact, I didn't know his end was so close. We stared at each other for a minute without saying a word, not even exchanging greetings as usual.

"Take this watch," he said as he pulled his watch from his hand. "Look for Aduke who is doing her national service in Bama in Borno State. She should be back in Lagos in a month or so. It's a pity she may not know about my case. Give her the watch."

He reached for his other pocket and brought out his car keys. I was nervous since his car was burnt by members of the Uvo family in the frenzy of that day nobody wanted to remember.

"Also give the car keys to Aduke. Whether my family likes it or not, my car's keys are for her," he told me.

We stared at each other and communicated the gloom ahead without speaking.

"Tell Aduke that I love her," he told me.

"It's not over yet, but I will convey your message if it is necessary," I assured him.

"I know you will," he told me.

For no reason we instinctively stretched out our hands and shook hands. I could not recollect any occasion in which we had shaken hands in our friendship. All our lives we had associated the shaking of hands with two strangers meeting, not with two friends. We were just too close to shake hands. And doing it as we were about to part, I did know it would be the last time we touched.

We heard about his hanging from the radio and I went with his family people to collect his body for burial. Ever since his burial, I have never gone to Okpara and I don't know whether I will ever go there again, except perhaps dead. I have disowned my extended family who I hear have also disowned me. I know they heard that I came to bury my friend, stood with his family, and did what was necessary for my friend to triumph in death over the forces he could not control while alive. My father has always come to visit me in Warri and does not mind my not coming to Okpara.

I located Aduke in Coker Street in Surulere and told her the entire story. She is still in mourning five years after.

the book case

Mrs. Fatumbi had innate poise and elegance. Her effortless beauty was like the moon radiating soothing brilliance. She learned intuitively that style or form, however fine, needs substance to be meaningful. To her, beauty itself is useless if it does not reinforce something else - character, talent, or some virtue. She knew that she was beautiful and attractive and did not need to go to the mirror to confirm it. Others have been her mirror. Before she married, what did she not hear men say? Hundreds of metaphors and images were used to describe and flatter her. She was a flower whose beauty surpassed imagination. She was an antelope, a goddess, *Mamiwata*. The compliments could make one lose one's head in the clouds and forget one's humanity, if you took them seriously.

What did she not see men behave like in her presence? She has watched men excited and possessed before her, but she neither encouraged nor taunted them. She understood human frailty. Did her father not once suggest that she should be a reverend sister? Even at her tender age, she wanted to live in the world and have some impact; so, she chose not to leave the world and go to the nunnery or to serve reverend fathers. She liked meeting people and teaching children. Her beauty never went into her head to make her vain. She knew from the beginning that she had a gift that she had to take care of humbly.

Her presence was always engaging. She wanted her brains

to be her identity. She did not want to be known only as "That very sexy woman!" or hear whenever she passed by only the exclamation "What a beauty!" She knew she was going to be a school teacher and not just an attractive female teacher, but the. brilliant one. She had her BS and MS in Geography from Vassar College, New York, where each semester she was in the Dean's List.

A beautiful and intelligent woman who has committed all her resources to academic improvement of Nigerian youths should be supported by all means. A woman who would forego the latest fashions in expensive "dressing to match" for writing an ambitious textbook for secondary school students should be applauded.

Five years of preparation of this Geography book was a period of constant sacrifice. All her savings from the United States went into it. She did not bring back many of the luxuries that academic returnees usually bring back from New York or London. What did she need a container of beds, chairs, cars, and other luxury items for? Some have brought back beds, as if the beds made in Nigeria were not good to sleep in. Many brought in Volvo and Mercedes cars, having decided that the Peugeot available in Nigeria was not comfortable enough to drive. Others brought in state-of-the-art stereo equipment. These luxuries were not her needs.

Her little savings from her earnings the past seven years added up to good money, but it was not enough to cover the cost of the two hundred and eighty thousand naira for the fifty thousand copies that were printed. A coloured textbook was a rarity in Nigeria and none existed in Geography. And still more unique, there was none by a woman.

The publishers had excitedly volunteered to "chip in" one hundred and fifty thousand naira. They suspected their author did not know that she had struck a gold mine. A much-needed and ground-breaking textbook in the famished land. They expected to reap a proud and rich harvest. The Principal of Akowe Secondary School who liked to be called "Provost" coughed out fifty thousand naira from the school's discretionary funds as loan to an industrious staff. He had no fears that Mrs. Fatumbi would have a windfall from the launching and sale of the book. Paying back the loan would be no problem, he judged. And there was the expectation of the West African Examinations Council adopting his staff's book as a required text. Apart from making his school well-known and the desire of every family to send their children there, this project could make millionaires of writer, publishers and patrons of *The Human Geography of West Africa*.

The few books published in Nigeria at the time sold out as soon as they were launched. They were all written on ex-Heads of State, ex-Chiefs of Army Staff, ex-GOC of Divisions, current leaders and their retinue of egoists. Many journalists jumped into the express business of writing autobiographies for pay. Uli Kalu wrote *Soldier Diplomat* and *A Time To Serve* for the President. The President who had just promoted himself to the rank of General, the highest military rank in the land, was compared to respected generals: Eisenhower, Westmoreland, de Gaule, and Nelson. Many Nigerians never heard of those generals, but they rightly suspected that Kalu was titilating the President's ego for pay. His rewards were publicly known as they could not be hidden. A house in the new capital, a Mercedes, and a million naira. Kalu made sure he engaged a friendly journalist to review the book in advance of the launching. It was declared a masterpiece by Professor Udo.

But the book that caught Nigerians off their pants was *The Home Frontline* by the First Lady, who by virtue of being "first" was also President of the Nigerian Army Officers' Wives Association (NAOWA). Her husband, the President of the

Federal Republic and Commander-in-Chief of the Armed Forces, was the Chief Launcher.

"On behalf of my Government, the Federal Republic of Nigeria, and myself, I launch *The Home Frontline* with ten million naira," he intoned through the microphone that echoed into local, national and international radio and television stations. He did not talk much as he believed that in book-launching, it was the amount of money you gave out that brought applause and not the high-falutin language you spoke. After all, he heard the story of the Professor who only gave his moral support and was asked, "How much money is moral support worth?" Trust Nigerians, they sneered at the learned Professor.

"Ten million naira and not kobos?" the audience questioned secretly in their minds.

But who dared violate their silence, now that silence itself had become the only means of protest by the poor and the powerless? Even the rich knew they were doomed in a country in which the President gave his wife ten million naira out of public funds. This would deprive some government hospitals of a much-needed maternity ward. It would prevent some towns from having their roads resurfaced. It would deprive villages of necessary potable water. It would deprive many of their lives. But as the elders who had grown philosophical said, "If the moon does not shine well, who would go to the sky to put it right?"

The co-launchers who were Government contractors knew they would have to give out hefty sums, but they did not anticipate that the President would raise the stakes so high. Government-appointed chairmen of companies, directors of oil corporations, banks, and other money-doubling industries who all owed their fat wealth to the Chief Launcher, each gave a million naira in cheques which they knew must not bounce if they were to retain their lucrative positions or even continue to live. How could they live without the appointments which they would even kill to retain? They knew the next budget would soon be out and they would do unto the President what he had done to them. The law of Moses had to be upheld.

The co-launchers knew that the President did not love his wife, but only wanted to show that he was the wielder of power in the country. Their only option could be to wipe out as much as possible of their department's annual votes to make up for this loss. The President knew this would happen, but he did not care as long as he pleased his wife after whom he had named a state. He had to close her mouth from complaining about his slipping out at night to have what he called security meetings in guest houses, but which she knew were rendezvous for his concubines.

After the realization of fifty million naira, there was a big toast. The bearded Minister of Culture talked of the creativity, imagination, talent, and genius of Her Excellency The First Lady, Dr. Hajjia Ogiso. After a spate of eulogies, some speaking in the past tense as if the woman was dead, the MC and Minister of Culture, known as the Federal Government Megaphone, asked all to stand. The Chief Launcher, co-launchers, unacknowledged writer, and all others present toasted crates of imported champagne to Dr. Mrs. Hajjia, who without receiving her doctorate in the conventional way, has produced an "epoch-breaking book of genius."

With such precedents of book launchings which were always blazed by the media, Mrs. Fatumbi felt her book, though a textbook, should do well. After all, the nation emphasizes the education of its youths. Parents would go any length to educate their children. The Federal Government and the various state governments always talked of supporting Nigerian authors who could write books that had a Nigerian flavour. Mrs. Fatumbi knew her book had a West African, albeit a Nigerian, flavour that would be difficult for any Geographer to match.

"As long as the book is well-received," she told herself "I will be all right."

She did not want to make a fortune out of the book. She would consider herself fortunate if she got back enough to write off her loans, the publishers' expenses, and to make up for all her own monies that she had sunk into the project. She realized that it would add up to a huge amount to reach this level, particularly since she did not have the clout of a First Lady, nor the talent to sing praises of the military, in spite of its ugliness, in newspapers, though this was the easy way of gaining recognition and government appointments. It was a public secret that the few women in Government were lovers to the President or to his few advisers.

"Nothing goes for nothing" has become a Nigerian saying among both children and adults. The irony was that the married women were members of the WAI Brigade whose much-advertised task was waging war against indiscipline. Lip service and pretence were fashionable virtues. Mrs. Fatumbi could not see herself, even for money or power, becoming one of those ducks! Many authors have gone out of their way to praise the Federal Military Government in the Foreword to their books, even though their books had nothing to do with politics, history, or government. Hers was an academic book, not the yellow journalism of *The Home Frontline* and others. Still, she was hopeful.

The invitation cards were specially designed by the female Art teacher of Akowe Secondary School. The printer made the cards beautifully glossy and very unique in the way it drew attention to the author and her book, the Chief Launcher and the MC. There were cards which though expensive were almost unreadable. But not this. The message of the launching was quite clear from a distance on the card. .

"I don't like this Frank Dede of a person to be publicly associated with you," the Art teacher had objected to Mrs. Fatumbi regarding his name being boldly displayed on the invitation card.

"His name is Dede Daro, not Frank Dede" Mrs. Fatumbi corrected.

The author knew that the tabloid materials on Dede's divorce and custody cases had done the distortion to such an extent that he was now called Frank Dede, after his former wife Franka.

"Why, my dear?" Mrs. Fatumbi asked back, unaware of any reason why Dede's name should not be there.

"You know this our country. Government is the provider for all and nobody wants to annoy Government. Frank Dede, I beg your pardon, Dede Daro and Government don't agree," Mrs. Toyin explained.

Nobody knew why she was called Mrs. Toyin. Toyin was her first name, but somehow she did not protest being called Mrs. Toyin. She wore a ring on her right fore-finger, but nobody believed she was married.

"But he is a brilliant journalist," the author insisted.

"Yes, but the launching is business, and I don't want anybody to pour sand into your carefully prepared pot of soup. In this country, people eat forbidden food in secret and wipe their mouths so that you will not know," Mrs.Toyin told her.

"You may like or respect him, but you don't have to let people see you with him in public or associated with your name in an important invitation card," she continued.

"Is that why some men will not greet an ugly woman during the day and at night steal in to sleep with her?" Mrs. Fatumbi asked.

"Of course, yes. No Government official or contractor will like to appear on television or in the newspaper sitting with Frank Dede, please forgive me, Dede Daro, the no-nonsense journalist. But it all depends on you. It is your book, not mine," she conceded.

"I have to keep my word. I approached Dede a long time ago to be the MC and he agreed. He has all along been following the writing of this book. I want the launching, apart from raising money to cover the production costs, to be a meeting of minds," Mrs. Fatumbi said in defence of her hand-picked MC.

"I hope the Chief Launcher, the publishers, and other invitees will enjoy the meeting of minds with Dede," Mrs. Toyin said, knowing she could not sway Mrs. Fatumbi to change her mind.

Mrs. Fatumbi suppressed her indignation at Mrs. Toyin, but was angry at the society that would treat a brilliant journalist as a pariah because he practically wanted to eradicate corruption as a national lifestyle. But she had to hold her head high as the chief hostess. It was her book and her business and she would stand for integrity.

Invitations flew into every corner of Lagos and the country, since education of young ones was taken as a national priority. Even if there was a lot of lip service in the country, it was only education, Mrs. Fatumbi felt, that rose above hypocrisy. You could see parents literally slaving themselves to send their children to school. Parents went the extra mile to meet the academic needs of their children and wards. Several nearby state governors, Ministers, Commissioners, secretaries and directors of education were invited, as were university academics, business tycoons, and well-wishers. Mrs. Fatumbi did not know all the people she was inviting and had not heard of some names until she set up a committee to suggest those to be invited. Some names she had read about in newspapers, others she has seen on television.

"You must be inviting the whole world," Mrs.Toyin told Mrs. Fatumbi.

"It will be an opportunity to bring all Nigerians together and highlight the importance of Human Geography in our national development," she explained.

"Are you going to put them in a house or a football field?"

"The National Theatre's Main Auditorium, of course."

"I hope you didn't take a loan for it! It will be a big crowd to serve drinks and snacks. Our people are fond of drinking and eating more than they donate," the inquisitive Mrs. Toyin remarked.

Mrs. Fatumbi and Toyin are friends, but the married woman keeps the single Toyin at some distance because Toyin has told her that she was ready to sell her body to make money, if need be, and when she has attained wealth, she would rehabilitate herself with a chieftaincy title.

Toyin was the devil's advocate, and Mrs. Fatumbi knew she needed her. Toyin always looked for the bad side of things, much unlike her who saw brightness behind the dark clouds. Now she had asked to know what she already knew: that she took a hefty loan for the launching. Added to her own money that she has already spent, she was neck-deep in debt and only a successful launching could rescue her from drowning in debt.

"You know that, Toyin; almost everything from the writing to the publishing and launching has been through loans," the author told her friend.

"May God help you," the alarmed Toyin said in prayer.

Toyin knew that Mrs. Fatumbi who was four months pregnant was exhausting herself physically and mentally. The author was individually responsible for preparations of the Auditorium and at times, she felt the huge hall would be too small for the education-lovers she was bringing in for the book-launching.

All the invitations were accepted, since nobody sent excuses. The RSVP was to Dede Daro who had received neither calls nor letters declining to attend the launching. Mrs. Fatumbi was happy there were no regrets.

On the Saturday morning of the launching, Dede woke to a brilliant sunshine. He felt the weather was an auspicious sign since there was no rain or cold to keep people away from attending the launching. Every activity in Lagos at the time was left to chance as the national television had abandoned its nightly weather forecast. The BBC and VOA gave weather forecasts for the day but it always came too late to be useful. This "August break" was a welcome break from the usual heavy rains of June and early July.

Mrs. Fatumbi did not have a restful night. She went to bed late in her attempt to put finishing touches to the arrangements. Dawn at last would bring the much-awaited day. She felt more excited and restless awaiting this book-launching day than she did on the eve of her marriage or the eve of her departure for studies in the United States more than twelve years earlier. She had long dreams, one after the other, in a few hours of sleep. In one of such dreams, she was being pursued by cows and she ran fast into a house that was policed by huge dogs that barked at her ferociously. She was surprised that she could run fast in spite of her pregnancy.

In another dream, rain beat her but she did not get wet. But the dream that worried her was the one in which she was dancing without her pregnancy and everybody was clapping for her. She did not believe in dreams unlike Mrs. Toyin and others who would go to fortune-tellers when they had bad dreams. But she was uncomfortable as she was more tired at dawn than before she went to bed.

In any case, it was the great day. Mrs. Fatumbi, the author, was at the National Theatre at 8 a.m. though the place was already arranged. She wanted no hitch at all. She had made copies of her one-page speech. She opted for a short speech as she wanted the book's content to speak for itself. Why should writers have long speeches after they have spent several years on a work? The book has its own mouth that would be sharper than hers. More so, she wanted to give time to the MC, Dede Daro, the reviewer, and the Chief Launcher to do the talking. She was not used to praising herself but she would allow encomiums on her work. Who says she does not like a little limelight, if it is to highlight her brains? All she hated is women who posed for nude photographs to be paid. She was baring her brains into the book that would be on display in bookshops and schools all over the country and possibly all over West Africa.

Dede arrived at 9.30 a.m., thinking he had come very early but only to find Mrs. Fatumbi sweating and cleaning the already clean floor. It was still one and a half hours away from the start of the great occasion.

"Mrs. Early Bird, you're already here," Dede teased her.

"Of course, I should be early bird this day of all days," she answered in a rather weak voice.

"I hope you slept well?" Dede asked, noticing the feeble voice of a usually vibrant woman.

"Not as well as I would have liked. Short and wakeful sleep, touch-and-go sort of sleep filled with many dreams."

"Don't be too anxious, it will soon be done. A market is terrifying at night when lonely. You seem to have entered a lonely market at night hence your bad dreams, if bad is what we can call them.

"Is your speech ready?" she asked her MC.

"Very ready. Only five pages. I have made some five

hundred copies for the important dignitaries."

"Will that number be enough?" she asked.

"Of course, you cannot give copies to every Nigerian. Only those who are likely to donate money and the press really need copies. We don't need to give copies to those who would not read the speech. At least they will hear it," he told her.

"You know these things more than myself. I am just a novice in book-launching," she admitted.

They laughed. One of the cleaners of the National Theatre peeped into the hall as if something sinister was happening.

"Una never start?" he asked.

"You de craze?" Dede shot back.

He relishes confronting stupid questions with stupid retorts.

"I beg una, I think say na here they say they go drink today. I fit get one bottle of beer from una? No be say una get money throw way?"

"Please leave us alone," Mrs. Fatumbi pleaded to the aged cleaner.

He left without further complaints, disappointed that the free-for-all booze he expected had not started.

At 11am, when the occasion was due to start, none of the invitees had come.

"When will we learn to be punctual?" Mrs. Fatumbi asked Dede.

"You don't know that not being punctual is an African disease?" he asked back.

"I hate this African time," she said loudly, as if she was talking to many people and scolding them.

"The leopard, you know, cannot remove its own spots. The spots make it what it is," Dede said.

Akowe Secondary School's Principal, the "Provost", came in, dressed in overflowing "up and down" robes. His driver carried his brief case and followed him like a personal servant and guard.

"The place is still like this?" he asked.

"They have not yet come," Mrs. Fatumbi said feebly.

By 11.30 a.m. the Publisher, his Sales Manager, and Public Relations Officer came in. They had thought they would come into an already filled house. The Publisher shook his head at the empty seats. He shook hands with the Principal and the Art Teacher. Soon it was 12 noon.

The waiting was silent and cheerless. The big clock on the wall began to tick loudly as if it had just started working. Its tick-tock became irritating to Mrs. Fatumbi. She went to the far end of the hall to sit down, her head bowed down. She closed her eyes, hoping she would open them to see the place transformed into a crowd. Once, twice, and thrice she tried it to no avail. She could not work magic. She closed her eyes tightly and wished she could block her ears to all sounds.

Dede felt he was in a nightmare. He has not had any since the court days when he slept little and dreamt a lot. At first he felt he would wake from the nightmare but it became an eternity. It was 1 p.m. Two whole hours after the occasion was supposed to have started. He began to doubt if the date was correct. He looked at his watch and it read the correct day. He looked out for Mrs. Fatumbi who was at the other end of the empty hall. He summoned courage and went to her.

"Let's postpone it," he told her.

Both knew they could not hide the failure. Somehow both of them knew without saying it that Dede Daro's name emblazoned on the card might be part of their current problem. But the deed was done.

Both Mrs. Fatumbi and Dede Daro went to the Publisher, "Provost," and Mrs. Toyin, who were sitting together but not talking. The silence between them had become heavy and they heard each other breathing heavily.

"We have to call it off for today. We can't launch this book today. If today were April 1 and not August 1, I could have felt it was a fools' day," Dede told them.

The publisher bowed into his voluminous dress, murmuring some words that nobody heard distinctly. They filed out leaving Mrs. Fatumbi, Mrs. Toyin, and Dede to do what they liked with the drinks and snacks meant for the launching. Their eyes were dry though cloudy.

A week later Dede still blamed himself for the tragedy. He was to be a witness in a very queer suit. He couldn't believe that Mrs. Eunice Fatumbi was dead. Life was so brittle it could snap anytime without warning when subjected to any undue pressure. Mrs. Fatumbi was really dead and already buried. The school teacher-author had been taken to hospital the evening following the abortive book-launching. She was pale and could hardly breathe, and when she did breathe, she gasped. She complained of a severe headache and blurred vision. Even when in hospital, the publisher came to her to complain about the money he invested on the book.

"That your book is my life. Something has to be done," he told a blank-faced Mrs. Fatumbi. "I will be undone. My company will be undone. All I have laboured for all my life will be ruined," he screamed at the wall, attending nurse, eavesdroppers, and all, except Mrs. Fatumbi who was only there in body but not in mind, were irritated by his insensitivity.

The publisher noticed that his author's case was very bad and that drove him into a delirious rage. When he started to wield a copy of the book like a matchet at the patient, the attending nurse felt she had endured enough of the madman's harangues. Mrs. Fatumbi was under her care and, considering the gravity of her case, she should not have allowed anybody close to her. The nurse summoned her energy and pushed Mr. Akin who fell on the floor. Everybody around stared at him in pity as if he was a madman. On the ground he started to stammer some words and foam in the mouth. The nurse held one of the poles that held IV water as if it were a shield. Everybody expected the madman to charge at the nurse or at Mrs. Fatumbi. The publisher gave a long look at the patient, stood up, and brushing aside people out of his way shouted that he should be left alone. Everybody kept a safe distance from him.

Upon Mrs. Fatumbi's discharge, the publisher's long letter was waiting for her. Her husband who had been away on business travel and the maid were careless in not hiding the letter from her. It was placed on her pillow and as soon as she was back, she saw the typed letter and knew immediately that it came from her publishing company. The letter was a diatribe against business done with women, worse with women like her who were too proud to obey men.

"There is no way you will have peace after ruining my life and my workers and my family who depend on me. You must be the worst bitch on earth, a cankerworm that needs to be expunged from the environment. You are too conceited to be intelligent, too clever to be marketable in any way. You are just a loser. . . " the letter rattled on.

She was barely two hours back when she had a relapse and had to be rushed back to hospital late in the night. That night she died of complications from pregnancy-induced hypertension, according to the doctors.

Before mourning was over, Mr. Fatumbi had sued Mr. Akin and his publishing house for five hundred thousand naira as compensation for killing his wife. The case itself was as bizarre as the death because if Mr. Akin were to be convicted for murder, the law would require him to be hanged or jailed for life rather than pay compensation to a living husband.

The papers had a field day as they had not seen since the Dede-Franka divorce-custody super case.

HUSBAND POISONED WIFE FOR MONEY
PUBLISHER MAD AFTER MYSTERIOUS DEATH OF FEMALE AUTHOR
JOURNALIST MESSED UP BOOK LAUNCHING
& LEAVES BEHIND DEATH AND CLAIM SUITS
MAN WRANGLES WITH DEAD WIFE'S LOVERS

The headlines were provocative and attention-grabbing. That was the practice of the papers.

Dede knew he had been tied in and he was perceived as part of the cause of Mrs. Fatumbi's sickness and eventual death. The painful thing was that she died with the baby in the womb. The doctors said they thought she would scale through the hypertension and have a normal safe delivery and so did not perform a ceasarian section to remove the child. Two people were dead from a failed book-launching. There were some papers though that put the entire blame on Mrs. Fatumbi herself and did not look beyond their noses. The *Lagos Weekend* put the tragedy at Mrs. Fatumbi's stupidity in not knowing that Dede Daro's name on the invitation card was a death knell for the launching. In a nation of praise-singers where people would genuflect in mud to a dog in power to gain favours, none was ready to be associated with the "insane journalist." How could one not guess that the State Security always trailed the journalist whose pen could expose the President who wanted to be respected abroad? Was Mrs. Fatumbi so dumb as not to know that the journalist MC was the bad luck that triggered the tragedy?

Toyin was given a centre spread, interviewed by the paper's social editor. She said that Mrs. Fatumbi was like a dog that was fated to be lost and so did not listen to the owner's whistle.

She had begged her to remove some names from the invitation card and invitation list but she would not listen. She got money from many papers, who sent people to interview her and later to make her say what they wanted to write to please their scandal-loving readers.

"I told her from the start that that name should be removed," she told one of her interviewers.

"Why did she not listen to you?" the female editor asked.

"She believed too much in herself and the worth of intelligence. She told me that the journalist was a very intelligent man and should be gainfully employed rather than left to write scathing articles against the Government."

"What a loss!" the interviewer exclaimed.

"There are very few of her kind and she died for her principles," Toyin lamented..

Dede would go to court again, but to be a witness to opposing sides of one case. Mr. Fatumbi expected him to corroborate his claim that Mr. Akin and his publishing company literally harassed and hounded his wife to death. He had a good attorney in the person of Dr. Titi Toko, Senior Advocate of Nigeria (SAN), one of the few female attorneys admitted to the highest court in the land. She was known to represent parties in which women had been abused or wronged and this was to be a test case of the society's exploitation and persecution of women.

The publisher also expected Dede Daro to be one of his key witnesses. He had sued Mr. Fatumbi, the deceased's next-of-kin, to pay back with "compound interest" the money loaned to Mrs. Fatumbi for the publication of her book. Mr. Akin had decided that the best form of defence is counter-attack. He had been sued and he had to sue.

Mr. Akin resolved not to hire an attorney to defend himself. He had lost so much money already and even if the case went against him, he had no money to pay however small the compensation that the judge might award. Had he not gone to court and seen how lawyers argue cases? Some were so weak that they did more harm than good to those they defended. And yet they had demanded heavy fees. Only the lawyer never loses, much like a fly that follows the hunter out in an expedition. Either way would benefit it, whether the hunter shot an animal or the animal mauled the hunter to death. Akin concluded he would have nothing to do with flies. Let them starve to death. He could defend himself. Mrs. Fatumbi was owing his company so much money and the widower wanted to forestall his asking him to pay back the late wife's debts. How clever some men are! He expected Dede Daro to sympathise with him and show that Mrs. Fatumbi exaggerated her ability to bring launchers to pay back the publishing costs. His case was self-evident and one did not need to have a lawyer to win it. Truth would be his attorney in the court and he would tell it to the world.

Dede had readied himself and his house for Furu's arrival and subsequent one-week stay with him. He had never felt as excited all his life. He swept the floors over and over again. He arranged the cushioned chairs neatly, placing the two-seater in a special position facing the television. This was the chair he hoped he and Furu would sit in most of the time. The bedroom had a flowery bedspread and the Queen-size bed appeared too small for two, but he felt the smaller it was the better for them to be close. The four weeks of expectation had passed so slowly that it looked like a full year. He had not expected that after Franka and the years of staying alone, he could ever be as excited as this by a woman. But there he was restless, his mind always fixed on Furu. He had framed her picture beautifully and set it by his bed. Whenever he was lying down in bed, he could see her on the wall. In fact, they stared at each other in the bedroom.

Now that the day he had waited for had come, he was more restless than when he was in the fifth form in secondary school and was expecting his first real date. They must be wrong, he told himself, who say that after a certain age that love no longer makes one mad. Love can make one mad at any age. Furu filled his thoughts and nothing else could interfere with the thought of her coming. He could see something of Furu to compare to whatever appeared before him The beautiful birds that flew overhead were Furu's maids. So were the stars; after all, she was the moon that made the entire night glow for him.

Furu arrived as expected. That night the migrating birds flew over his roof in the moonlit sky. The birds were heading from the dry Sahel towards the southern evergreen forests. They kept each other awake with recollections of their childhood and did not realize the night was far gone till there was a cockcrow, a rare thing in Lagos. Looking at the wall-clock, they saw it was already four o'clock.

They had barely started to sleep in the morning when there was a strange knock on the door at about six o'clock. The knock was hard as if the person knocking was desperately trying to get into the house, perhaps escaping from chasing dogs or robbers. There was a kick on the door and a loud "Are you hiding from me, Dede. I am Akin, I am still alive and you can see that I kick hard."

Dede knew from the voice that it was the publisher but was surprised that he chose such an early morning to bother him with his complaints.

"Just wait, I'll open the door for you," Dede shouted to him outside.

He went back to the bedroom to wear something more decent than his split night gown. As he came back, there was another bang on the door.

"I've seen you, open the door for me," Akin shouted as he fumbled with the door knob.

Though Dede felt something was amiss, he realised that opening the door fast would be better than delaying. Furu had got up and followed him to the door. When the door opened, they could see from Akin's bloodshot eyes, unkempt hair, and rattled appearance that there was trouble.

"Come in," Dede told him as he moved aside for him to pass.

"No, I will not enter your house until this case is finished," he shouted as if the person he was talking to was not beside him.

Akin dug his feet by the threshold and refused to move.

"Do you know how I can get a copy of the woman's American certificate?" he asked Dede.

Dede knew that he meant Mrs. Fatumbi and could not pretend not knowing who Akin meant.

"I have never seen her certificate," he answered.

"I went to the Records Office and got her death certificate, that will do. Whatever earlier one the husband got, mine is as good as his," he blurted.

Dede almost asked what he was going to do with Mrs. Fatumbi's American or death certificate, but thought the better of it because he knew that Akin was not in his right mind.

"You are not of any help, but let me see you in court tomorrow," Akin said and turned to go.

Furu accompanied Dede to court. Dede was firm that he could not bear false witness against anybody, more so against the late Mrs. Eunice Fatumbi. He regretted his past when he lied against Franka to win the divorce and custody cases. But he would no longer debase himself. He had the highest regard for the woman who had been so brilliant and industrious. It was a shame that the society did not recognize her worth and indirectly contributed to her death.

The Fatumbi case against Akin was the third in the order of the day. But that order could be accelerated or delayed according to the wishes of the presiding magistrate. Mr. Fatumbi was already there by the time Dede and Furu arrived. They greeted him, but went to sit at a different side. Akin had not yet arrived. He had become strange and might take his time to come.

The first two cases went very fast and by nine-thirty it was the Akin case.

"The next case is the Book Case," the judge said. He adjusted his white wig and smoothed his black gown, the paraphernalia of justice. He bent down to write for a few minutes and when he finished, whispered something to one of the court police.

"Mr. Akin!" shouted the police.

He was not around. There was silence, as the judge found it unusual for the party claiming damages to be absent.

"Mr. Fatumbi!" the court police shouted.

"Yes!" he responded.

The judge started to write again. He wrote very fast, his head bent low as if he did not see well enough except from a close range.

"This case is thrown out for lack of merit. The accuser is troubled and out of his mind and since he cannot show up in court, his case is hereby dismissed. The counter case is also dismissed. Mr. Fatumbi, you owe nobody any money for your wife's death or book business," the judge read from his big book.

"Order!" shouted the court police.

Mr. Fatumbi stepped out with a squeezed face. Dede and Furu went to congratulate him and the children who accompanied him to court.

"In fact, I saw Mr. Akin this morning as we came to court. He was picking pieces of paper from the street. I think he is really insane. It's a pity, but I have also suffered," he told Dede.

The book-publishing deal and the abortive launching that led to Mrs. Fatumbi's death were a sore area to talk about for all concerned. The two did not have much else to talk about and they said goodbye and left for home.

Only two years after Mrs. Fatumbi's death, *The Human Geography of West Africa* was adopted as a required text by the West African Examinations Council for its high school final examinations. The publishing company, in the absence of Mr.Akin, made enormous profits from which over the years it paid Akowe High School its loan. The remaining money was shared between the company and Mrs. Fatumbi's children. From their share of profits, the publishers took psychiatric care of their former manager, Mr. Akin. Today every high school geography student in West Africa knows Mrs. Eunice Fatumbi, but not to the extent to which her book they read tells them anything about her death or the related madness.

as in such things

One late Friday evening, he came to my home. The heavy downpours that menaced our evenings were gone for the year. The dampness of the rainy season that kept people at home was also gone. In its place there was a cool breeze that could have come from either the direction of the ocean to the south or the harmattan winds to the north. Already we were looking forward to the harmattan winds and their accompanying cold. At the time of his arrival, my wife and I were watching a children's programme which would soon give way to the local news in pidgin English at seven o'clock. Before, during, and after the local news, came announcements of obituaries, installations of chiefs, parties, and so much that defined our social lives. We cherished ceremonies and the television and radio that made so much money from our egotism fed us to the throat with their announcements. People paid the exorbitant price for the announcement of a death on television without any complaint. They borrowed to have burials, but neglected the children of the deceased who might need assistance.

I was very surprised at how my visitor got to know where I lived. I had known him casually for a year or so. He was a fairly tall man of moderate build, the sort of man who should have been an athlete or football player in his youth. Fair in complexion, rather like a mixture of black and red, he showed signs that he was already losing much of the lustre that might have enriched his skin in earlier days. But he was no longer young, being now in his late fifties, I supposed.

I didn't even know his name. He came to my petrol station to buy fuel regularly, and once in a long while bought Super-V engine oil and asked my boys to change the filter and oil. We exchanged greetings because of his familiar presence at the petrol station, but we did not make any effort to know each other beyond these fleeting greetings. But here he was in my home, somewhat familiar and at the same time strange to be seen here. Of course, being my customer, I gestured to him to take a seat, which he did, facing me. I then asked for what type of drink he would like to take.

"Anything will do," he said.

There were some bottles of Star beer left in the fridge from the previous day's stock. I got up and asked my daughter to bring the beer and a glass. As I got up, he protested.

"Oga, I no wan give you trouble. You be chief, don't get up."

"Don't worry," I told him, "you are my guest."

My guest took his beer slowly as we concentrated on the commercials and the local news.

The television announcer had started the litany of obituaries in the familiar words:

"With gratitude to God for a life well-spent, we are happy to announce the passing away of our father, husband, friend, and people's chief, Chief Orie, aged seventy. He is survived by fifteen children, twenty-eight grand children, and two wives. Burial arrangements will be announced later. Signed: Dr. Kevwe Orie, for the family."

Other announcements of death, some by accident, followed. At this time, my guest cried out, "But this life na waya-o. Small pickin de die like fowl."

I suspected there was a reason for the toad to be jumping

about in the daytime. And he knew that I was expecting him to divulge why he visited, though that would not have been necessary if we were more familiar or if we were friends. Friends popped into each other's homes without prior announcement. He appeared to struggle within his mind about what to say. My wife left, feeling that her absence would encourage the visitor to state the purpose of his coming. It did. What had been choking him came out. He wanted a loan badly. I didn't even hear how much he wanted.

Of course, as in such things, the instinct is to say, "I don't have anything myself, even if one had." It just happened, however, that what I told him was almost true. Business was very slow with the frequent fuel scarcity. Unlike independent distributors who could adjust their prices of kerosene and sell their petrol in drums, we, the oil company distributors, were forbidden to cut corners to make profit. The law of supply and demand did not work in our business. I relied on the commission I received from selling the fuel I was supplied and my tanks were dry. I was already finding it very difficult to pay my workers. My children in the university and in secondary schools were back home to get money for their fees and subsistence. Things were very hard, I told him. A hen had gone to a cock to ask for eggs, I said, because I felt my responsibilities were heavier than his.

We continue to be shocked by strange happenings. As soon as I declined his request, his face fell down and he burst out crying. This man whose name I didn't still know was past middle age. I had not experienced a fiftyish or sixtyish-year old man weeping so helplessly. I was sure I was much younger than he was. Again, as in such things, I kept quiet for a moment, and then I asked him to be calm.

"How can I be calm?" he asked.

"What's the matter?" I asked back.

It was then that he told me amidst sobs about the two or more stones he carried in his heart. His friend from childhood was seriously sick--I didn't ask him the kind of sickness. I respected his keeping private what his friend suffered from. But his friend desperately needed money to be flown overseas for medical attention, without which there was no hope of survival. But his dilemma was not just trying to help a friend, but he was heavily indebted to him. As the care-taker of his friend's house in Warri, he had collected the year's rent. He was allowed to use the money in his business until the now sick friend in Benin would need it. He lived in a two-bedroom apartment in the four-apartment storey building. He did not want to be responsible for his friend's death, more so after all the kindness he had shown him. He said what pained him so much was that his friend's wife would hold him responsible should the man die.

"How can I live with the thought of killing my best friend?" he shouted absent-mindedly.

His friend's wife had come to tell him of his friend's urgent need. He told her that he would get things together and come to Benin to see his friend the next weekend. The wife took this as a firm promise.

He talked about the other stone he bore in his heart. At home, his eight-year-old son was sick. He had no money to take him to the hospital, and all he was doing was praying that his case should improve. So far the case was bad but was not getting worse. A medicine store owner had been selling him drugs on credit to treat his son. He could not afford to take the child to the General Hospital, where the consulting doctor would need a bribe before checking a patient whom he would advise to seek help at his private clinic. In Warri, you needed three thousand naira or more to get treatment for even cold or malaria. How could he afford this when he could barely take a full meal once a day?

I was not a rock. Even rocks could melt from heat. Sometimes we forget our own problems when we weigh them against the magnitude of other people's. His sobs and story melted me. He wanted fifty thousand naira. I went into my bedroom and took out the fifteen thousand naira I had put aside for my children's upkeep. I did not think about how I would send my two children back to school.

My wife came back to take her seat beside me. She must have been in the kitchen and getting ready to set the table because we normally had dinner about eight o'clock. By then, my guest had put away the money I loaned him. It was in her presence though that he promised to pay back in March. Early November to March was only about six months. After then, he left.

My wife asked what I had done and I told her only half the truth. I couldn't tell the full amount I gave out. But she suspected in my reticence to tell her that I had done one of those dumb things I would be ashamed to discuss with her.

"Who is he?" she asked.

"I don't know his name," I told her.

"And you loaned him so much money?"

"Not too much," I said.

March passed without my seeing the man. In the interval since September, I no more ran across him buying fuel or engine oil in my petrol station. I didn't catch him any day servicing his Peugeot 504 as he used to, once in a long while, at the station. I put it that, after all, I had only met him by chance, and I didn't spend all day there. Perhaps he still patronized my petrol station and it just happened that I didn't happen to be around when he came. Somehow, more than at any time before, I wanted to see him and ask him about his Benin friend and his sick son.

At the end of June, I made inquiries to know his name and his address so as to go and find out why this man whom I perceived to be honourable had not shown up as he promised. I wanted to know how he was faring. Frankly, I needed money too, but I just wanted to see him. I was anxious to know what happened to an older man who burst into tears because of his needs before a younger person. From my description of him and his car, one of the mechanics in the station's workshop recognized him and the area in which he lived. I now knew his name. Nick Mara. He lived in Pesu Street in Odion area. My cousin, Auntie Rosie, lived in the same predominantly Itsekiri quarter by the river; and I had visited her many times.

My people and his people had always been embroiled in land feuds and had many times these past twenty years fought with casualties on both sides. And yet from the beginning, we had been very close, like a couple who always quarrelled but could not do without each other. We inter-married and gave each other's names to our children. Outside Warri, who knew the difference between Itsekiri and Urhobo? After all, we call them Irhobo, a name so close to ours. But this discovery of Nick's background made me desire more to see him. He had come to me as one who knew another man and that pleased me. He was not Itsekiri to me and I was not Urhobo to him in an ethnically divided city.

I drove to Odion by Pesu and parked my car by the roadside. Pesu Street was not a long street and ran into Market Road. When I came to what fitted the description of his home area, I asked a man about him. The man knew him very well, pointed at his house, and went his own way.

Nick Mara's car was not there. He had gone out, but his wife was home. Rather pale, with the trace of a once-beautiful body, Mrs. Mara was a little agitated when I asked of her husband.

"How are the children?" I asked.

"Fine," she said weakly as one who did not care about what she answered.

"Tell your husband that his friend who owns a petrol station and lives in Agaga Layout asked of him. I would like to see him sometime."

"Is that all the message?" she asked.

"Yes."

The building had not been repainted, and the peeling original paint gave the house a dull brownish ochre-like appearance. The inside was mouldy, the cushion-chairs cumbersome and smeared with sweat. Some were torn and I could tell that their springs were either broken or loose. I knew that Nick Mara was not yet doing well, at least financially from the look of his home. Anyone who had such a fine woman as Mrs. Mara would use his means to make her shine, but she looked like a star covered by clouds.

He came to me in the evening the day after my visit to his house. I was expecting all or part of my money.

"My wife told me that you came. I apologise that I wasn't home when you visited," he told me.

"Don't worry. After all, I didn't inform you that I would call at yours. I only took a chance," I said.

"That doesn't mean. I am sorry to be out," he said as if pleading.

Before me was another absurd scene. He knelt before me and begged to be given more time.

"Get up first. Nick, get up! Don't curse me by kneeling before me. I think you should be my senior in age and you can't kneel before me, no matter what," I told him.

"Oga, I don't mean to curse you. I can't curse you," he explained.

"Okay, get up!"

He got up, sat down, and continued to apologise profusely for disappointing me. As in such things, I told him not to worry. He looked haggard, his beards unshaven. You could tell he had a great load on him, and I didn't want to exacerbate his plight.

A month later, I went to pay a condolence visit to him. His son had died. While there, I learnt his friend who could not be flown abroad for treatment had also died. His car was parked, dry of fuel. His wife and relations were more afraid of what would happen to him in his distraught state than they were concerned about their mourning for the dead son and friend. His head bowed, the people talked to his ears.

"You don't have to kill yourself because of the dead."

"Take care of your wife and the other child, rather than all three of you to die."

"What is ahead is more important than the past."

His people and mine have always been neighbours and we knew each other's customs. I gave him five hundred naira and asked him to come to fuel his car on my expense at my station. He raised his head, stood up, walked to me and shook my hand. Life had to go on despite losses.

the wake-keeping

It is only those who lack experience about life who argue that certain things can't happen. Anything is possible. Once something, however strange happens, it becomes an experience. Precedents are set by strange occurrences. I now know that every story is true or capable of being true. This was what I came to learn from what took place in my own Okpara. The big family wanted to do their best to bury their own, but the man's own children ruined the whole thing.

All sons-in-law and their friends assembled for the wake-keeping and burial of Odova. His house was small by Okpara standards for a man with many children. He did not live all his life in shame. He would have been the only man with grown-up children living in a thatched house in his quarter of Okpara but had been saved from shame fifteen years earlier by one of his sons-in-law who paid for the roofing of the house with corrugated iron sheets. The mud walls were plastered with cement and given the appearance of a house built with cement blocks. The roof had now rusted from the frequent rains of the area. He was going to be buried in a house of corrugated iron sheets rather than in a hut, what the people called a home roofed with thatches. He was saved from one shame by this son-in-law's kind gesture.

The sheds outside were made of palm fronds. Odova was a poor man and his several children were not doing well. The crowd was small. The townspeople who hungered for wake-keeping in order to drink, eat, dance, and flirt their fill did not expect much from this one. There were no invitation cards distributed. Everything was by word of mouth. Relations had not come from afar. It is doubtful if the family found it necessary to send one of theirs to Yorubaland or Hausaland, where some of their people lived. The family knew they had double standards in their practices--one for the rich and the other for the poor. None of Odova's children complained because there was no money to send one of them to invite their distant relatives, who would not leave their works anyway because of Odova's death.

Preparations were made for the wake-keeping and burial as in the days before the newspaper, radio, and television. There is a proverb which says that one can measure with one's eye the pounded yam that can fill one's stomach. Most Okpara people measured Odova's wake-keeping with their eyes and saw nothing to leave home for.

The people who gathered were somber rather than celebratory as was common in such occasions in Okpara. After all, Odova was old, about seventy. He had several wives, but had lived with one as far as many Okpara people could tell. The women who were expected to sing dirges were quiet like the men. No one expected a motorcade as in other burials. None of his male children had left the town, they had all remained scratching a living. An only son, Odova had only half-brothers and half-sisters, none of whom had a car or car-owning friends. His first daughter sold tomatoes in Igbudu market. Her husband who had been doing well had had a stroke and was bed-ridden. The other daughter was married to a greaser, who sold engine oil in gallons and quarts and greased cars for a pittance. The third daughter who had run from home lived with a messenger in a secondary school in Sapele. All three were there with their husbands and friends. A few motor cycles and many bicycles were parked around.

When Odova died in Ufuoma Clinic in Warri, the senior

daughter felt the easiest way for her then was to ask the body to be kept in the clinic's morgue until she had informed the family on what to do. She did not think of the daily fee for keeping the body there, a fee that was more than any of the deceased's children's monthly earnings. The children had expected the death because of the rare nature of his sickness.

The family held a meeting after the senior daughter cried home to report the news. She had told her brothers and sisters who were all summoned home about their father's body in a mortuary in Warri. None of them took into consideration the fee for keeping the body there when they agreed to tell the bigger family that their father should be buried in a month's time.

The family meeting was controlled by the elders and not Odova's children. Orise, the family elder, supported by other elders, fixed three thousand naira as the total amount to be contributed. Every adult knows that a man's children, not his relations, village or town, bury their parent.

"You don't age for the village or family but for your own children," Orise reminded the assembled family. Others concurred.

The children kept quiet when the family split the three thousand naira, which would not even be enough to buy fish to prepare palm oil soup, not to mention the drinks and the other items of entertainment. In the children's thinking, one did not need to flaunt poverty before the extended family. They wanted to maintain some sense of pride and honour. On their part, the elders could not ask the family they knew to be poor to contribute more.

The contribution was like a struggle to squeeze juice from a dry fruit. Very little of the shared money was contributed. When asked for their share of two hundred naira, the Okite branch of the family complained of hard times, sick ones in the hospital, and other responsibilities. The family was able to find only one hundred and twenty naira.

"What's important is contributing something. Here's my share, this amount," another said.

He did not mention the mere ten naira he contributed. Everyone knew that with that type of pittance, nothing could be bought. Things had become so expensive that hundreds of ten naira could not make a dent on whatever they wanted to buy.

As the sun set, more people trickled in. Not the big crowd that characterized expensive burials. The scanty crowd exchanged pleasantries as was customary and no one expected any lavish ceremony, nor the turn of events they would remember for the rest of their lives.

"The dead is dead, and the living have to deal with life. Let us drink," the town-crier said.

He attended every wake-keeping in town. He took as compensation for his role of alerting the town of news to participate in every public ceremony that provided free drinks and food.

"Bring the drinks," an elder shouted, as if he had cartons of beer or soft drinks in stock somewhere.

The family drinks were not many and had been kept under lock until late in the night. The children had calculated that the sons-in-law and their friends would bring out their drinks and that should carry the assembly on for some time. They, children of Odova, would formally entertain people after the corpse had been brought.

It was cool, the sun had set. Night was falling. People were looking out for the pickup van that was to bring the corpse from Ufuoma Clinic. The senior son had left for Warri since three o'clock. He had chartered a pickup van from an Okpara driver living in Warri and had also made arrangements for a coffin in Warri, the extended family had been told.

In the half light of early nightfall, a pickup appeared. Once the van's lights appeared, there were sighs of relief as the waiting had become too long. At last, the body has come, they felt. The van came to a stop. In the dark, one could not see what was inside.

But instead of the first son to unload the pickup van of its coffin, he strolled to where the elders sat.

"They have refused to release my father's corpse," he told them.

The elders listened with bewilderment. How could a morgue refuse to release a corpse to the family claimant? The first son did not wait to be asked why. He could see on their faces that they wanted to know why the impossible had happened.

"The money I took there wasn't enough to pay the charge," he told them.

There was a murmur among the elders, so loud that it drew the attention of the scanty crowd.

"Every day the strangest thing happens," the oldest man said to the hearing of those sitting around him.

The word soon went out and round. Odova's children could not pay the hospital bill to recover their father's body. After the initial consternation, sons-in-law, well-wishers, and the extended family swallowed the news quietly and behaved as if nothing unusual had happened. They knew that wretchedness made one to do shameful things. They continued the wake-keeping, but without the corpse for the women to dance around.

Still they drank. The sons-in-law brought out their cartons of drinks. The children brought out their drinks. No musician was brought, but the sons-in-law had brought boom boxes and played Urhobo dance music. The young and old danced. The flirtations that usually took place at such nights took place but on a very low scale.

Most of those who came from outside stayed through the night because of rampant armed robbery. They were stuck with the wake-keeping till dawn. By the second cock-crow, it was dawn enough to slip out. Nobody went to the deceased's children or family, as was the custom, to say words of comfort. The sons-in-law took their wives and their own children with them when they left. By the early morning there was no corpse to bury.

Meanwhile the mortuary fee was escalating and nobody knew when Odova's body would be recovered.

"If that body is ever recovered, I won't come to another burial ceremony. I will give one excuse or another," the frail husband of the tomato-selling daughter of Odova said.

"What will happen if the children, extended family, or townspeople are unable to recover the body?" one woman asked.

"Let the clinic burn the corpse!"

The few people around the speaker seemed to have agreed to this simple solution. Nobody felt offended.